Today

TODAY

Book Three of the Yesterday Series

A Novel By

Amanda Tru

Published

Sign of the Whale Books™

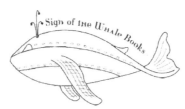

Sign of the Whale Books

Today
Book 3 of the Yesterday Series

Second edition. Copyright © 2015 by Amanda Tru. All rights reserved. No part of this publication may be reproduced or transmitted in any form or by any means — electronic, mechanical, photocopying, or recording — without express written permission of the author. The only exception is brief quotations in printed or broadcasted critical articles and reviews. This book is a work of fiction. Names, characters, places, and incidents are either the product of the author's imagination or are used fictitiously. Any resemblance to actual events, organizations, places, locales or to persons, living or dead, is purely coincidental and beyond the intent of either the author or publisher. The characters are productions of the author's imagination and used fictitiously.

PUBLISHED BY: *Sign of the Whale Books™**, an imprint of *Olivia Kimbrell Press™*, P.O. Box 4393, Winchester, KY 40392-4393. The *Sign of the Whale Books™* colophon and Icthus/spaceship/whale logo are trademarks of *Olivia Kimbrell Press™*.
*Sign of the Whale Books™ is an imprint specializing in Biblical and/or Christian fiction primarily with fantasy, magical, speculative fiction, futuristic, science fiction, and/or other supernatural themes.

Original Copyright © 2013.

Cover Art and Graphics by Debi Warford (www.debiwarford.com)

Library Cataloging Data

Tru, Amanda (Amanda Tru) 1978-
Today, book 3 in the Yesterday Series/Amanda Tru
  202 p. 20.32cm x 12.7cm (8in x 5in.)

Summary: When tragedy strikes, will Hannah be able to face a today without her happily ever after?

      ISBN: 978-1-939603-75-3

1. time travel 2. christian romantic mystery 3. new adult 4. male and female relationships 5. parodoxes

[PS3568.AW475 M439 2012]
248.8'43 — dc211

TODAY

Book Three of the Yesterday Series

A Novel By

Amanda Tru

TABLE OF CONTENTS

CHAPTER ONE

I felt muscular arms around me, and my heart skipped a beat. Waking more fully, I felt the warmth of Seth's bare chest on my skin and the slight whisper of his breath on my cheek.

His eyes were still closed in sleep as his body rose and fell with slow, gentle breaths. Strands of my own long, auburn hair reached across the white pillow to his wavy blond.

In awe of this beautiful creature asleep beside me, I gently caressed a line from his muscular upper arm all the way to his fingers.

He was mine.

Faint gray light crept around the edges of the drawn curtains as I watched Seth sleep and memories of yesterday flooded over me. I was Seth's wife! We had spent so much time anticipating, planning, and preparing. Yet in the end, it had happened so fast that my mind couldn't wrap around the fact that I was now Mrs. Hannah McAllister.

The ceremony had been mid morning, followed by an

outdoor luncheon reception. Always expecting the worst case scenario, I still couldn't believe everything had gone so seamlessly. Our families, extended families, and friends had all attended. My sister, Abby, had been my matron of honor, and Seth's best friend, Wayne, had been his best man. My dress fit, the rings didn't get lost, and I managed to repeat my vows without crying or stumbling over the words.

But, best of all, with love in his blue-green eyes and no hesitation, Dr. Seth McAllister had said, "I do."

The reception was held at Seth's parent's house in Pacific Grove, and, at their insistence, my new in-laws had spared no expense in the lavish party. The California summer weather was beautiful, making the ocean view breathtaking. I was told that the catered luncheon was delicious and the wedding cake unusually good. I think I ate a few bites, but I was too excited and busy greeting everybody that the taste never registered. Wayne caught the garter, and my bridesmaid, Natalie, caught the bouquet. Leaving the reception was a bit like trying to navigate no-man's land as showers of rose petals and birdseed bombarded us. Making our escape in a heavily bedecked white Rolls Royce, we drove directly to the airport to catch our flight to Hawaii.

All in all, it was perfect—maybe even too perfect. Events in my life have never seemed that easy, and part of me was a tiny bit superstitious that everything really was too good to be true.

Arriving on the island of Kauai before dark, we checked into our room at the resort and didn't leave. We had saved intimacy for our wedding night, and it had been worth it. The wait had made our wedding night more special, more intimate, more passionate. I felt my face heating up with the memories.

The thought of Seth's love for me was overwhelming. I loved Seth so much that, at times, it felt like a physical ache. But that was understandable. Seth was a handsome, highly successful doctor with a line of ladies wishing for any encouragement. I was just a lowly wannabe artist who came dragging a long line of strange problems. Seth's gentleness, his fiery kisses, and his words of passion all spoke of a deep love for me that I couldn't seem to understand.

I had never imagined an intimacy that was so exquisite. In Seth's arms I felt cherished, and yet I also felt a passion I never imagined myself capable of. The feel of his warm skin and taut muscles beneath my fingers was something I would never tire of.

Awed by my newfound freedom and unable to resist, I lightly ran my fingers over Seth's back and down his arm again. He stirred but didn't wake.

I wanted to wake him and make sure I hadn't just imagined last night, but I reluctantly decided to let him sleep. The poor man had been putting in long hours helping with wedding preparations as well as tying up research at the Tomorrow Foundation.

On the other hand, I couldn't continue torturing myself by lying so close to a gorgeous man I shouldn't wake.

Carefully, I extracted myself from Seth's arms and crept out of bed. Slipping back on the slinky white negligee that had been decorating the floor, I also grabbed the matching sheer thigh-length robe.

Tiptoeing to the heavy curtains covering the patio

doors, I moved one aside and peeked out. The beautiful morning view of the ocean made me catch my breath. Unable to resist, I unlocked the sliding door and quietly slipped out to the private patio.

Although this fourth floor patio was partially enclosed for privacy, I still stayed close to the shadows. My attire wasn't really appropriate for any audience besides Seth. I'd change clothes and come out for a longer time later, but, at the moment, I simply couldn't resist the view.

Though not directly facing East, pink streaks still extended across the sky from a fading sunrise, intermingling with blue and reflecting on the dancing waves past the beach. Breathing deeply, I inhaled the smell of the ocean and the rich, fragrant aroma you can only find on a tropical island.

I was on my honeymoon! My wedding had been beautiful! The man of my dreams—my husband—lay sleeping in my bed!

I couldn't stop smiling. It was a moment I wished I could keep forever. For at that one snapshot of time, I was utterly and supremely happy.

I stood for several minutes, breathing deeply and enjoying the intoxicating happiness course through me as I watched the pink streamers in the sky slowly fade to blue. The spell was finally broken as I became chilled from the slight breeze and my lack of apparel. A nice warm bed, fully equipped with a hot husband sounded entirely too tempting.

If Seth just "accidentally" woke up, I could always just apologize later.

I quietly slid the sliding glass door open, moved aside

the curtains, and slipped into the room. Before I made it three steps, two pairs of eyes looked up at me from the bed. Neither one belonged to Seth. A man and a woman had obviously been enjoying their privacy in what was supposed to be my bed. Both were wearing less clothing than me.

Shock hit me like a jolt of electricity, and I let out a strangled screech.

The woman began shrieking and clutching at the blankets. The man grabbed at the phone beside the bed and started pounding buttons.

"I'm so sorry!" I said, my body shaking with shock and confusion. "I must have the wrong room!"

I don't think they could hear a word I said over the woman's continuous high-pitched screams. The man was yelling into the receiver, saying there was a crazy intruder in their room and demanding that Security be sent immediately.

Panicking, my only thought was to get out of there fast. I dashed for the door and ran into the hall. I heard the man yelling for me to stop. Turning right, I ran without thought, expecting to be tackled by burly security guards at any second.

CHAPTER TWO

I reached the elevators and stopped, watching the lights slowly blink on and off as the elevators reached other floors. An elevator wouldn't reach the fourth floor in time, and, even if it did, security guards might be inside.

I heard voices.

Frantic for escape, my eyes snagged a door to the left marked with a plaque reading 'Maintenance.' The knob turned under my fumbling hand, and I shut myself into the pitch black closet.

I closed my eyes. *Just breathe,* I told myself, trying to calm my racing heart and prevent the sobs that threatened to choke me. Not sure if my wobbly legs would hold me much longer, I crouched and put my head on my knees.

What just happened?

But, deep down, I already knew the answer. I hadn't made a mistake. That had been my balcony, my hotel room, my bed. But, they obviously weren't mine *today*.

Could this really be happening, again?

It had been over a year since I'd last time traveled.

Ever since, I'd been faithfully taking daily medication to prevent the chemical imbalance in my brain that triggered the time travel. I'd never missed a dose.

This wasn't supposed to happen!

Despite the confusion as to why, I realized time travel was the only explanation. I had stepped out on that balcony in my own time, and I had reentered the room in either the past or future.

Voices seemed to stop directly outside the closet.

"Are you sure she came this way?"

"She ran this direction, but I don't know where she disappeared. She couldn't have gone far." I couldn't be sure, but I was guessing this voice belonged to the man from the hotel room.

"What did she look like?" I figured this must be a security guard,

"Young with long, reddish hair. She was wearing some kind of white lingerie with a robe-thing over the top."

The security guard laughed. "If she's running around the hotel dressed like that, we can't miss her!"

The voices moved down the hall and I exhaled. They were right. I wasn't going to get far in my white teddy. I suddenly recalled a conversation I'd once had with Wayne about the fact that, when I time traveled, I seemed to take with me anything I was physically touching at the time. I guess I should've been grateful that at least I wasn't completely naked.

What was I going to do? It wasn't safe for me in the hotel. If I got caught as the crazy intruder, there was no way I could explain my actions. I wasn't even currently a guest at this hotel. If I did manage to escape without being caught, I needed to find a way to relax enough to trigger my time travel back to where my husband was probably freaking out. And, I had to accomplish all of this without doing something that would drastically and forever change the timeline.

First things first. If I was going to be inconspicuous, I needed to find something to wear. I had no clothes, no ID, and no money. *Think, Hannah, think!* Wracking my brain, I finally remembered reading in the guest info that the hotel offered a full set of amenities, including complimentary hotel robes and towels for use when enjoying spa treatments or the pool. If I recalled correctly, these were available in the locker rooms on the first floor. If I could make it there, I could possibly swipe a robe until something better came along.

Before leaving my maintenance closet hideout, I located a light switch. I had hoped to find something useful, maybe even a uniform of some kind, but there was nothing but a cart holding a myriad of cleaning supplies.

As my mind flittered through possible plans, I figured the absolutely worst case scenario would involve me trading my lingerie for a simple pool towel. Then I could claim that my clothes were stolen while I was showering. Maybe someone would then have pity and loan me some clothes until I could "return to my room and get my own."

After turning out the light, I opened the door to an empty hallway. I knew taking the stairs would be safer than an elevator, and, sure enough, I located the door for the stairs across from me. Scampering across the hallway, I opened the door and listened for any footsteps echoing through the cement cavern.

Hearing nothing, I entered the stairwell and flew down the cold steps as quickly and quietly as my bare feet would allow. I had to make it to the first floor before encountering anyone else. Halfway down the second flight of stairs, I heard the ominous echo of a door opening and slamming below. Then heavy footsteps plodded my direction.

Heart pounding and feet skipping down the rest of the steps, I made it to the second floor landing. The door protested with a loud echoing screech as I hurriedly opened it and pulled it shut behind me. I hadn't been seen, but I still wasn't safe. The person on the stairs might only be going to the second floor. He or she might open the door at my back at any second. I needed to find a place to hide.

Suddenly, I heard other voices coming toward me from around the corner.

I was trapped!

Seeing a large conference room door across from me, I acted without thought. The knob turned in my sweaty palm, and I slipped inside the room.

It was already occupied.

Hearing voices, I slowly turned around, fully expecting exclamations of shock at the sudden interruption from a half-naked woman. But there was no reaction. With relief, I saw that I was well-concealed by a huge fichus tree that was directly between me and the other inhabitants of the room

Turning back to the door, I thought I might be able to open it a crack and watch for the owners of the voices in the hall to leave. Hand on the knob, I stopped, recognizing a vaguely familiar voice behind me.

"I really don't think such drastic measures will be necessary," a woman's voice said. "There's no real cause for alarm yet. I'm really only telling you this as a courtesy."

"A courtesy!" A man's voice sputtered in sudden anger. "You're our lawyer, and you're in this just as deep as we are! If we go down, you're coming with us!"

The curiosity was too much. I knew that woman's voice. I just couldn't place it. Releasing the doorknob, I crept forward and carefully peered through the leaves of the tree. Recognition was immediate.

Katherine Colson.

Katherine sat at a large conference table with three men in suits. *What was she doing here?* Katherine's face was the only one I could see through the leaves. Not wanting my movement to attract attention, I gave up on getting a better angle and just listened to the heated discussion.

"The methods you are referring to will provide the nails for your own casket," Katherine replied in a cold, steely voice. "If, however, you follow my advice, you and the company will be protected against any future discovery."

The man actually snorted.

Katherine continued. "Right now, we don't know who he's told about his research. He only discussed it with me because he considers me a friend and wanted to know the legal ramifications. He has no idea you're my client. If you do what you're hinting at and kill him, more people will become suspicious and add credibility to his research."

"You underestimate my methods," the man replied. "No one would suspect foul play or connect his unfortunate accident to his research."

"And you underestimate who you're dealing with," Katherine shot back. "He's smart. He has a partner who very likely knows every inch of the research. There are other people personally and professionally that he's close to. You have no idea what he's already figured out. He might have fail safes set up in case of an 'unfortunate accident.'"

The man started to reply, but he was interrupted by one of the other men who had been silent until now. "So, Miss Colson, this whole situation sounds potentially devastating to our company, yet you say there is no cause for alarm. If you don't think the situation warrants Mr. Durst's solution, what is your advice exactly?"

"His research is in the beginning stages. But, even if it goes nowhere and no threat comes of it, chances are that someday the information you are carefully guarding will come to light. If not through this doctor now, then through a different doctor in the future. I really believe our best way to survive this scenario is to play dumb. Your own research never indicated the medications had any potentially hazardous side effects. You had no idea. Lawsuits and criminal charges will come if it is discovered that you knew about the problems and did nothing. If you didn't know, and you have a paper trail to back up your story, we will just have to deal with a recall. You already have been given FDA approval, so any lawsuits would go nowhere when pitted against the government and your own extensive research showing the drug was safe as far as you knew."

"But we have no such research," the man replied. "We have the opposite. Even though we have carefully tried to delete and cover up the research, our actual paper trail would be devastating if discovered."

"That's why we need to get to work now," Katherine urged. "Documents, e-mails, research—everything can be forged. And, a person with the right skills can make it appear that the unfavorable information never existed. The desirable documentation can be inserted in its place. Everything will appear legitimate."

"You're talking about a massive internal covert investigation and cover-up. Where are you going to find someone who is part spy and part computer genius? Much of the evidence can only be planted by hacking computers, probably including some external to the company."

"I will find someone," Katherine replied, but even I thought her confidence sagged for the first time.

Mr. Durst snorted again. "It can't be done. It's too complicated," he said adamantly. "We'll deal with other potential threats in the future. Right now, we have to neutralize this threat."

The room was completely silent for about thirty seconds. Finally, the third man spoke in a quiet, almost timid voice.

"Miss Colson. We will, for now, try to follow your advice. You will be tasked with finding the appropriate employee to fill our requirements. If you are unable to meet our unique needs, we may have to resort to Mr. Durst's methods. Let me also assure you of one other thing, my dear. Durst is right, if we go down, you will go down with us."

I had never heard a serious threat delivered in such a sweet, unassuming voice. The contrast sent chills down my spine.

Katherine gathered up her papers and walked toward the nearest exit. Fortunately, it was not my door.

"Oh, and Miss Colson," the quiet voice called gently. "We don't want to ignore the current threat while preparing for the future. Please keep us apprised of the progress made by our good Dr. Seth McAllister."

CHAPTER THREE

SETH? They had been talking about *my* Dr. Seth McAllister? I had been so intent on listening to the conversation that I hadn't stopped to wonder about the identity of the person they were discussing.

My breath caught and goose bumps spread over my entire body as I replayed the conversation in my mind. They were talking about killing him!

Feeling the panic rise, I tried to take deep breaths and remind myself that this was either the past or the future. They hadn't killed Seth… yet.

Before I could process any more, my eyes caught movement. Looking through the leaves, I saw the three men heading my direction. Quickly turning the knob on the door, I exited the room, pulling the door shut behind me as softly as possible. Terrified of running into Katherine and knowing that the three men were on my heels, I saw the maintenance closet for this floor and scurried inside.

As soon as I shut the door, I heard voices, but they were too low and muddled for me to understand. This closet smelled so strongly of disinfectant, it was overwhelming. As I held my breath, I tried to sort any meaning from my chaotic thoughts.

Had Seth discovered something potentially dangerous in his research and not told me? He had obviously told Katherine.

When exactly was I? Was this something that had already happened or would it happen in the future? I certainly didn't recall any research that might get Seth killed. He hadn't had any "unfortunate accidents" either.

Then I remembered. The mugging.

Seth had almost been killed a year ago. With information from the future, I had been able to stop what had been labeled as a random mugging. The assailant had fully intended to kill Seth. At the time, we had thought some of the details about the attack too strange to be random, but we dismissed them after the police investigation. Now I wondered. Had that been a hit hired by the men I'd just overheard? But, there hadn't been any more attempts on his life since then, at least none that I knew about. Had Seth known he'd been targeted and purposely kept information from me?

One thing was clear, I needed to get back to my own time and interrogate Seth myself. From previous experience, I knew the only way to reverse the direction of my time travel was to relax. This would cause a sudden decrease in the neurotransmitter, tempamine, and send me back to my original time. Unfortunately, I was also aware of the dangerous side effects that would await upon my return.

Feeling like I was going to pass out from the fumes and lack of oxygen, I opened the maintenance closet door a crack and peered out. The hall was deserted once again. I just had to make it down one more flight of stairs and find the ladies' locker room. If I was going to have any hope of relaxing in my present circumstances, I was going to need clothes.

Finding the stairwell quiet, I quickly crept down the cement steps to the first floor. I knew this next leg of my mission was going to be more difficult. How was I going to get through the busy lobby of a luxury hotel and not be seen?

Opening the stairwell door a sliver, I scanned the lobby. To my relief, it was relatively empty. A couple was standing at the front desk, three people were close by waiting for an elevator, and everyone else appeared to be in the lounge section at the front of the lobby with their backs toward me. If I could time this right, I just might make it.

A door screeched open and closed above me, its echo sending waves of dread through me. Heavy footsteps stomped down the steps.

Come on, elevator! Come on! I urged, practically hyperventilating.

Finally, I heard the happy ding of the arriving elevator.

Closer and closer the footsteps came.

The three guests moved as if in slow motion, boarding their transportation and painstakingly selecting their buttons of destination. The elevator doors lazily drifted shut, and I flew out of the stairwell. Trying not to break into an attention-grabbing sprint, I walked quickly to the back of the lobby toward the pool. Thankfully, the map of the hotel was still fresh in my mind, and the concierge stayed distracted with his guests.

Hurrying outside to the pool area, I immediately wedged myself in the shady corner by the door and hid behind some convenient tropical foliage. I had a direct view of the door to the women's locker room. Beyond that, I could see the glistening blue of the pool. Seeing no one in the near vicinity, I acted quickly. Scurrying out of my hiding place, I dashed for the door and pulled the handle.

It didn't budge. Locked!

Panicking and realizing I was now in plain view for anyone in the pool area, I abandoned the door and ran back to my hideout behind the door to the lobby.

Taking deep breaths, I tried to steady my shaking hands while my mind frantically searched for a Plan B. As I watched the door to the locker room through fern-like leaves, a woman walked up and slid a card into a slot above the handle. Easily pulling the door open, she disappeared inside.

The card she had used had looked like the same key card used to open a hotel room door. I thought about trying to steal or "borrow," someone's key card, but then dismissed it as too dangerous. Watching the door, I suddenly realized that if I timed it right, I wouldn't even need a key card.

I watched as another woman slid her card into the door and entered. Hurrying forward, I reached out to grab the door before it closed. But before I could grab the handle, the door opened again, almost hitting me in the face.

A woman and a young girl walked out. Headed toward the lobby, they passed mere inches from where I had my back plastered against the wall. Fortunately, the open door partially hid me, and the mother and daughter never looked my direction. The door beside me slid shut with a thud. Traumatized by the near miss, I retreated back to the foliage.

A few minutes later, I had regained my composure enough to try again. Giving up was not an option. Getting in that locker room was still the only plan I could think of for getting some clothes and ending this nightmare.

I figured the safest option would be to follow someone going in rather than out. There was less chance of being seen if I could just slip in the open door behind someone. I saw a blond woman exit the lobby and head for the locker room.

Now was my chance.

She slid her card, opened the door, and entered.

Waiting a full second, I sprang forward. Sprinting the few steps, I reached my hand out to grab the handle a split second before the door latched.

Suddenly, I felt hands on my shoulders jerking me backward. My fingers never touched the silver metal of the handle. The door thudded shut once more.

The hands on my shoulders pulled me back toward the corner that had been my refuge. Twisting, I tried to identify my assailant, but I kept losing my balance as my feet struggled to keep up with the reverse direction. Once behind the fern leaves, the momentum stopped and the hands released me. I whirled around.

"Hannah Kraeger, what in the world are you doing here?" Natalie Bishop stared at me, her eyes wide in shock. As her gaze raked over me, her next question was more of a shriek. "And what the blazes are you wearing?"

Opening my mouth to explain, I paused, confused about how to explain my current circumstance.

"I—"

"Wait!" Natalie held up her hand, interrupting before I could even start. Closing her eyes, she swallowed and took a deep breath.

My mind still reeled over seeing my friend in such an unexpected place. With my own question as to what she was doing here on my lips, I suddenly remembered Natalie's unexpected and bizarre trip with Katherine to Hawaii. That trip had been a year ago. Now, I wondered exactly how much Natalie knew about Katherine's dealings here in Hawaii. Did she know Seth was in danger?

I quickly dismissed the thought. Natalie didn't know anything. She had been my roommate until I married Seth. She was the most loyal person I knew. There was no way she would keep quiet if she knew Seth was in trouble. She intensely disliked Katherine, and I'd never been able to figure out exactly why she had agreed to go on this trip with her anyway.

At least now I knew exactly *when* I was.

Opening her eyes and looking at me again, Natalie finally continued. "Never mind. Don't answer those questions. I don't want to know. Just tell me why you need in the locker room."

"Clothes," I said miserably. "I have no clothes, no luggage, and no hotel room. I was trying to get into the locker room to beg, borrow, or steal something to wear."

Natalie stared at me for a long moment. I saw the

questions in her eyes. I would have told her everything. But she didn't ask.

Instead, she said, "There are about twenty little girls and their mums in that locker room right now. They just finished a special swimming class for kids. I was lying on a beach chair by the pool when I saw you trying to sneak into the locker room. Hannah, if you go in there dressed like that, you'll probably be arrested for indecent exposure and have a line of wealthy ladies wanting to sue you for scarring their innocent little girls."

I bit my lip to keep it from quivering. I felt grateful that Natalie had prevented me from causing such a scene, but I also felt completely despondent at the hopelessness of my situation. Nothing was going according to plan.

"Wait here," Natalie said. "I'll be right back." Walking to the locker room door, she slid her card in and turned to look back at me. "Don't move, Hannah," she ordered sternly.

A minute later, Natalie was back with a bag on her shoulder and two beach towels in her arms.

"Wrap this towel around your shoulders like you're cold," Natalie directed as she handed me a towel. "Good. The towel completely covers your clothes, or lack thereof."

"Thanks," I said, still feeling miserable.

"I have clothes you can borrow in my room," Natalie said as she wrapped the other beach towel around her own waist. "We'll just head up and get them."

"That might be a little tougher than you think, Natalie." I confessed. "I was sort of in the wrong room and startled a couple. Security is looking for me."

Natalie stared at me for a long moment, but didn't ask a single question.

"All right, then." She finally replied. "Just follow my lead, and we'll make it. Confidence, Hannah. Head up. Act like you belong here."

I knew that would be easier said than done.

"Chocks away!" Natalie said under her breath as we entered the lobby. I looked at her sharply. Natalie reverted to British colloquialisms when she was nervous or emotional. Other than her British phrase for "here we go," Natalie gave no other sign that she was concerned in any way.

We were almost to the elevator when we were stopped by a young man in a suit.

"Ladies, we do have a fully equipped changing room by the pool if that would be more convenient."

As I tried not to shirk and look guilty, Natalie took over.

Making a point of looking at the young man's hotel name badge mounted on his suit, Natalie replied in her most Britishly superior tone. "No, Trevor, it would not be more convenient. The ladies changing room is currently occupied by dozens of young girls and their mums. Now, if you'll excuse us, we prefer to use the privacy of our own 'fully equipped' rooms. Unless that is a problem?"

His face turning slightly pink, Trevor hurriedly stepped out of our way. "No, no, go ahead."

As the elevator door shut off our view of the lobby, I sank against the back wall.

"Natalie, you are absolutely amazing," I breathed.

"Save your compliments until after we make it to the bolt-hole," Natalie replied.

I made a mental note to ask Natalie later for the exact definition of the term "bolt-hole." Nevertheless, I got the idea that Natalie was still extremely nervous. When Natalie pressed the button for the fourth floor, I thought I might get sick. Knowing my friend was probably at maximum stress capacity, I didn't mention that I was a wanted fugitive on the fourth floor.

Please, Lord! Let us make it to Natalie's room! Don't let anyone recognize me!

The elevator doors slid open, and I followed my friend down the hall. Natalie quickly rounded a corner with me at her heels.

"Ooonph," She grunted, running headlong into someone coming the opposite direction.

Having no time to put on my own breaks, I ran into Natalie's back.

"Perhaps you'd better be more cautious about racing down the hall," a cool voice spoke as Natalie recovered from an assault on two fronts. I immediately recognized the voice for a second time today—Katherine.

"Perhaps you should follow your own bloody advice," Natalie snapped back

"I'm not the one in a hurry." Katherine replied calmly, smoothing out her purple designer suit with her hands. "Where are you off to at such a reckless pace?"

"It's really none of your business Katherine," Natalie said, her sweet tone only emphasizing the harshness of her words. "Now if you'll just excuse me…"

"What is *she* doing here?"

CHAPTER FOUR

THOUGH I had tried to remain hidden behind Natalie, Katherine had spotted me anyway. And her response was true to form. She had never liked me and usually, rather pointedly, ignored my presence entirely. If she did so happen to acknowledge my presence, she would never directly address me, acting as if I wasn't actually there or intelligent enough to respond myself.

"Again, Katherine, I really don't think it is any of your concern," Natalie answered sharply.

"It is my concern, Natalie. Now tell me why *she* is here when she's supposed to be in San Francisco. Just a coincidence? I think not."

Natalie and Katherine were at a stalemate. Katherine was insisting on an explanation for my presence, and Natalie wasn't going to offer her the lint off her towel.

"Actually, it is a coincidence," I said, feeling the need to speak up myself. "I came on this trip unexpectedly. I only later found out that this is the same hotel where you and Natalie were staying."

"And why exactly are you here?" This may have been the first time ever that Katherine had talked to me directly.

My mind spun, trying to come up with an explanation that would satisfy Katherine.

"It was an unexpected family emergency," I said, which in a way was true. My genetic abnormalities caused my time travel. That would definitely be an unexpected emergency caused by my family.

"I wasn't aware you had family in Kuaii."

"I guess we're all full of surprises," I replied, my eyes locking into hers, meeting her challenge with my own.

Katherine glared back at me, refusing to look away. As I looked into her eyes, I wondered what other secrets she was hiding. She had been trying to protect Seth, but why? She was obviously involved in some major illegal activities. From the conversation I had overhead, it sounded as if she was representing a company who knew their product was causing harm. And yet she was assisting them in covering it up.

I suddenly found myself locked into a staring contest with Katherine. I was not going to be the first to look away. She was the one who should be ashamed. Even knowing that her clients had tried to kill my husband, she still chose to do nothing.

Almost as if she could read the accusations in my eyes, I saw an unidentifiable emotion flash through hers, and she looked away, breaking the tension. After the space of a few heartbeats, she then looked back at me once more, a pleasant, serene mask now firmly in place.

"Just remember to stay out of my way," she said. Though her voice was sickeningly sweet, her threat was obvious. Without waiting for my reply, she brushed past Natalie and me and continued toward the elevator.

After a few choice descriptive words said under her breath, Natalie grabbed my upper arm and practically dragged me down the hall. Stopping at a door on the left, she quickly inserted her card, opened the door, and pulled me inside. Wordlessly, she pulled a pair of shorts and a shirt out of her suitcase, and pushed them into my arms.

"Thank you," I said softly as I took the clothes and changed in the bathroom. Natalie's clothes weren't exactly a perfect fit, but definitely an improvement over what I had been wearing. As I came out of the restroom, Natalie was dressed in a classic black business suit and staring blankly out the glass sliding door.

"Natalie, I really need to explain things," I said softly. "If you're going to help me, you need to know what's going on."

Natalie swung around and literally put her hands over her ears. "No, Hannah! Don't tell me anything! I don't want to know!"

"I don't understand," I said, completely bewildered by my friend's behavior. "You're my friend and my roommate. I'm sure you know by now that something is going on!"

Natalie removed her hands from her ears, but looked at me with a pleading expression, "No, Hannah, please don't tell me. Of course I know there's something strange about you. I'm not an idiot. The same day we first met at Silver Springs, you suddenly disappeared, and I didn't see you for the next three years! Then you have all these unexplainable health problems, and of course, every day I see you taking those pills that Wayne gave you."

"Aren't you even a little curious? You've never asked a single question, and now you don't want me to tell you at all? I need your help, Natalie!"

Natalie looked at me, and I saw her swallow. "Just tell me what you need, Hannah, but give me as little information as possible. If I don't know, I can't be made to tell certain people who shouldn't know."

Natalie's eyes were filled with misery, and I felt a chill as if ice water had suddenly been dumped over me.

"Natalie, what exactly do you mean?" I asked, my tone wary.

"I didn't even want to come on this trip, but Katherine has certain leverage that she can use against me. She's done it before. If I don't know anything about you, she can't make me tell."

"Natalie, what leverage? Is Katherine blackmailing you? I thought you accepted her offer to come to Hawaii because you lost a patient."

"That's what I wanted people to think. But even losing a patient wouldn't be enough to make me join forces with her." Natalie sighed and flopped onto the bed. "I don't know that you can call it blackmail. I don't come from a wealthy family. The only way I was able to attend medical school was because of the generosity of a family friend. Years ago when my family moved to the US, my dad got a job in a factory. It's a factory Katherine's family is heavily invested in. When Katherine asked me to assist as an expert on one of her cases, I refused. Though it seemed legit, I would never trust Katherine to represent the honorable side in a case. She then insinuated that she'd heard they were getting ready to make cuts at my dad's company, and she certainly hoped my dad wouldn't be one of those who had to leave, especially since he is so close to retirement."

I'd known some of Natalie's family history and even met her parents a few times, but she'd never shared anything like this before. I'd known that Natalie had moved from England to the US before she was a teen. While her family had loved living here, they had never been wealthy. Natalie had gotten a good education, and even spent considerable time back in England, courtesy of a generous family friend.

Natalie continued, "Even though I understood exactly what Katherine was saying, I thought she was bluffing, and there was no way I was going to bow to her threats. Then my dad mentioned that one of his supervisors came and asked him some strange questions, like about how soon he was planning to retire. He's worked there for almost twenty years! He can't lose his job! So I told Katherine I'd be her medical expert on this one case."

"Oh, Natalie, I'm so sorry! You should report her to the police!"

"For what? I have no concrete evidence. And that would really insure she would seek revenge on my dad. A few times Katherine has asked strange questions about you. So far, I can honestly tell her that I don't know. I really don't want to be put in the position of trying to hide something from her. If I can just bide my time for another six months, Dad will retire. If Katherine wants me to do something illegal, I'll refuse, of course, but until then, I'll have to cater to her for a little while longer."

No wonder Natalie had never asked questions! She'd

been trying to protect me!

I felt so helpless! The more I found out about Katherine, the more I felt she was pure evil. But the only way to stop her would be to help Seth uncover the mess she was in with her client. They had said that if they went down, Katherine would go down with them. Now I had even more incentive to get home to my own time and tell Seth what I had discovered.

"Thank you for trying to protect me, Natalie. I won't tell you anything until you are free to ask me. For right now, I just need to relax somewhere. Do you have any ideas?"

"Well, you are in Hawaii," Natalie said with a smile. "It's ironic that after all of Katherine's pressure to get me here, she hasn't even needed me yet. She had some big emergency meeting with a different client that flew in unexpectedly. So I've gotten to enjoy my stay here a lot more than I anticipated. I just have to be at Katherine's beck and call."

As if on cue, Natalie's cell phone rang.

"Speak of the devil..." Natalie muttered right before answering the phone.

"What do you want, Katherine?" Natalie asked in greeting. She paused. "Fine. I'll be right there."

"I've been summoned," Natalie announced after hanging up the phone. "I have to go be an expert."

"Natalie, I may not be here when you get back," I said. "Maybe I should say, I hope I won't be here when you get back."

Seeming to understand, Natalie nodded. "I guess you

should go relax then."

Sometimes I wondered if Natalie understood more than she let on.

With her hand on the doorknob, I called, "Oh, and Natalie…"

She turned back around to look at me.

"When you get back home, we probably shouldn't talk about my little unexpected visit. In fact, pretend I wasn't here and don't breathe a word to anyone about it. When I can, I'll bring up the subject… in about a year."

After Natalie left, I felt at loose ends. I wandered aimlessly around the room, inspecting the décor and even the coffee pot in the corner. I hate coffee.

I picked up some tourist brochures Natalie had left on the little table next to the coffee pot. Instead of giving me ideas for relaxation, leafing through them just left me depressed. I had no money to spend for any of these relaxing excursions in paradise. Besides, I had been looking forward to experiencing such Hawaiian adventures with Seth. I was supposed to be on my honeymoon, and yet, in this current time, that honeymoon wouldn't even occur for another year!

I sighed, feeling my tension increase—the opposite of what I needed. I considered lying down on the bed to try to sleep. That had worked before. Something in the process of my muscles slowly relaxing into sleep had always been enough to begin reversing the chemical responsible for my time traveling and send me back to my correct time. Unfortunately, as I looked at the bed, I realized I probably had more chance of encountering a penguin on the Hawaiian beaches than I had of encountering sleep in an unfamiliar bed, in an unfamiliar time, and with an unfamiliar enemy possibly plotting to kill the man I loved.

Beaches. My eyes swung to the sliding glass door that exited onto the room's small balcony. The hotel sat right on the beach, making the panoramic ocean view a mere stone's throw away. Turquoise water gently lapped the golden sand in regular waves outlined in white. As much as I hated the idea of leaving the safe harbor of Natalie's room, I could feel the beach beckoning me with a gentle pull. I realized it might be my best and only option.

I quickly left the room before I could give myself the chance to overanalyze and freak out with anxiety. The door clicked shut behind me with an unnerving finality. I had no key to get back inside the room.

I took a deep breath. Confidence. That's what Natalie had said. I had to pretend that I belonged.

But despite my internal pep talk, I couldn't make myself look in the eye any of the people I passed. I kept expecting to be stopped by security. Would I be recognized? I made it to the elevator. My heart was pounding. I put my back against the corner as another couple joined me for the trip down to the lobby. Fortunately, they paid me no mind, exiting quickly once we reached the ground floor.

Stepping out, I glanced around nervously. Katherine should be in the meeting with Natalie. I really did not want any chance of running into her again. This time she might be more insistent about her interrogation.

Relief poured over me as I stepped out into the warm sunshine. Kicking off Natalie's flip-flops, I picked them up and made a beeline for the water, the warm sand squeezing between my toes. As I reached the wet sand of the shore, I began walking, breathing deeply of the slight, salty breeze and feeling the cool foam of the waves creep up around my ankles and recede, only to return once more.

After about five minutes of walking, I stopped. There weren't as many people on the beach here as there had been right in front of the hotel. I slowly turned a full circle. This looked to be the right spot. At least, the trees and the few rocks looked familiar.

Taking a few steps back up into the warm sand, I turned back to the ocean and sat down. I probably should have grabbed one of Natalie's towels, but at the moment, I didn't mind the feel of the sand as I burrowed my legs in the warmth and watched the ocean's regular breathing. In and out--soothing in its predictability.

Three hundred and sixty-four days from now, I would be sitting in this exact spot with my husband's arms holding me close. I slowly lay back, allowing my hair to blend with the sand and cradle my head in its soft cushion. Closing my eyes, I remembered what was, for me, only last night.

After arriving in Hawaii, Seth and I had checked into our hotel, eaten dinner, and then taken a walk hand-in-hand along the beach. Finding this spot away from other tourists, we had sat and watched the sunset. Though we weren't directly facing west, the setting sun to our right still sent magnificent wide brush strokes of bright orange across the sky. As we watched, the oranges had slowly darkened to purple.

I breathed deeply of the fresh, salty air, remembering how Seth's masculine scent had mingled with the slight breeze. The sound of the waves was almost hypnotizing.

Warmth from the sand gradually crept over my body, wrapping me in the peaceful cocoon of that exquisite moment. My limbs became heavy. In that stage in between sleep and awake, I could feel my body, but it was almost as if I was floating up from it, swept away in the memory that was once again real.

I could almost feel Seth's presence beside me.

And then I heard his voice.

CHAPTER FIVE

"HANNAH, I'm here. Hold still."

My eyes flew wide. Startled, I sat up, immediately wide awake. The sun's bright glare momentarily blinded me, and I groped at the sand, my fingers instead encountering Seth's form kneeling beside me.

"Seth! Are you really here? Am I back? I have to… I need to…"

"Calm down, Hannah!" Seth ordered. "I will answer your questions right after I give you this injection."

My eyes cleared, but unfortunately my mind did not. At the sight of the long needle I began instinctively scooting away from it.

"Hannah, hold still! If I don't give this to you right now, you're going to be in intense pain and pass out in a matter of seconds!"

But even as he said the words, pain shot through my head with nauseating force. I plopped back in the sand as if being knocked over. Though I remained conscious, I was only vaguely aware of Seth giving me the injection in my rear.

Without a word, Seth then sat on the sand himself and pulled me into his arms. I tried to speak, but couldn't. Instead, I watched Seth's blue-green eyes as they did their silent assessment of my condition. I could see the shadows of worry and questions, but he remained silent, waiting until the medicine took effect and I could actually respond.

As I looked at him, an emotion stronger than pain forced its way to the forefront. Fear. Someone had tried to kill this man I loved, and though it had been a year since then, I had no assurance that they wouldn't try again.

I couldn't handle the thought of losing him. I took a deep breath and closed my eyes, saying a simple prayer asking that God take the fear away and replace it with peace. God had protected him thus far, and the sooner I recovered from this latest episode, the sooner we could talk and develop a plan. Right now, I couldn't take the chance of getting upset and losing my grip on this time yet again.

I focused on breathing deeply and relaxing in Seth's arms, feeling the medicine slowly easing the pain by degrees.

Finally, I opened my eyes, reached my hand up, and caressed the rough stubble of his cheek. "How did you find me?"

"I woke up and you were gone. I searched everywhere. When you were gone for over an hour, I was pretty sure you'd time traveled. I knew you wouldn't go anywhere without at least a note saying where you'd gone. But it isn't as if I could announce to the world that my wife had disappeared and mount a large-scale search. I knew that, if you really had time-traveled, you would have to relax in order to make it back. I also knew that, if I didn't find you to administer the Karisenol right away, you would probably die. So I've been walking the beach, thinking that you'd probably come here to relax. Knowing we'd come to this spot and watched the sunset, I figured this might be where you'd show up. I've been praying nonstop since I woke this morning. If I hadn't found you right away…"

Seth stopped speaking, the worry in his expression never lessening as he seemed to make a visual assessment. "Feeling better?"

"Yes. Much"

Seth suddenly stood, and with me still in his arms, began walking back down the beach.

"Seth, what are you doing? Where are we going?" I had expected him to be intensely relieved at my return and then immediately launch into an interrogation of where I had been and what had happened. This silent, resolute Seth was unexpected.

Seth didn't respond to my questions but instead kept walking. As much as I loved being in my husband's arms, I wasn't going to let him carry me all the way back to the hotel. While I wasn't overweight, I wasn't exactly petite either. "Seth, please put me down. I really think I can walk by myself."

"No. I am not going to put you down." He finally responded, still holding me securely. "That injection I gave you isn't a cure. It'll last long enough to get us back to the hotel. Then I'll have to give you repeated shots until your body readjusts the tempamine levels."

"But I'm fine right now, and it's a long walk back to the hotel. If you don't let me walk at least part of the way, *you* might not make it."

Seth stopped and gently put me down. "I think you're overestimating your weight and underestimating your husband's muscles, but if you insist…"

I slid my arms up to wrap around Seth's neck. "Trust me. I am fully aware of your muscles and all their many talents."

I had just time traveled and evaded death once again. The least he could do was act a little happy to see me. I gently kissed his lips. My heart accelerated as he immediately pulled me to him tightly, responding hungrily. At the desperation in his kiss, I understood how scared he'd been, how scared he still was.

Seth pulled away and looked down at me with heavily lidded eyes that failed to mask his worry and pain. "What happened, Hannah? Wait. Don't answer that." Seth closed his eyes and took a deep breath. "Let's talk about it back at the hotel. We need to get more Karisenol into your system."

I somehow got the impression that the medication wasn't the only reason Seth didn't want to talk about it yet. He was afraid for some reason. He was either afraid of why I had time traveled and what I had experienced, or he was afraid that something in the retelling of it would be too emotional for me. He and Wayne had always thought I was more apt to time travel again right after returning. They had always been protective to the point of the ridiculous when I returned. They had made everyone walk on eggshells around me and even tried to keep me sedated.

As Seth took my hand and we began walking back through the sand, I felt a fresh wave of helplessness wash over me. The daily medication I faithfully took was supposed to prevent me from time traveling at all. It had given me my life back. I no longer needed to fear experiencing emotion, and those around me no longer felt the need to protect me from reality. I was never supposed to time travel again!

And now… that specter had once again returned to shadow my every thought. To make me and those around me live in constant fear.

This wasn't supposed to happen. Seth and Wayne had assured me it wouldn't happen.

I suddenly stopped, my gaze swinging to my husband. "Wait a minute, Seth. Why do you have Karisenol with you? I thought the Hannahpren I take every day is supposed to prevent me from time traveling. Why would you bring the Karisenol on our honeymoon?"

Seth couldn't look at me, faltering at the accusations in my gaze. Instead, he took my hand and urged me to keep moving.

"I'll answer your questions, Hannah, but only if you keep moving. I don't know how long that dose I gave you is going to last."

I obediently resumed walking, trying to ignore a slowly intensifying headache.

Seth sighed. "Wayne and I have always known there was a chance the Hannahpren wouldn't work forever."

"But you didn't tell me?"

"No, we didn't. Just the possibility that you can time travel and end up dying is a major stress. And since stress and emotion trigger it in the first place, we thought eliminating the threat, at least in your own mind, would be one of the best ways to prevent it from happening."

"So you lied to me? Did you give me a placebo to take every day as well?" I could hear the tension tightening my voice.

Seth stopped and put his hands on either side of my face, forcing me to look him in the eye. "Hannah, you cannot get mad at me right now. Focus. Keep calm. You can get mad and yell at me all you want later."

Knowing he was right, I tried to breathe evenly and force my stressed muscles to relax. I didn't like that he had withheld information from me, but the man had just saved my life... again. If he just wasn't such a wonderful hero, I could get seriously angry at him!

Seth put his arm around me and began propelling me forward again, not willing to waste any more time.

"We did not lie to you. Hannahpren is not a placebo. It does keep you from time traveling. It's been over a year since the last instance. But this is a medication Wayne and I created. It has had little to no testing, even if we did actually have a way to test it. We're not sure what it will do. We knew there was a possibility that your body would develop some resistance to it. Like many medications, the longer you've been on it, the more your body requires in order for it to remain effective. We chose not to tell you—not to worry you over a possibility we couldn't verify. I always carry Karisenol with me, just in case something like this happens.

"Everything is going to be okay. I have enough with me to get you through this episode. When we get back home, Wayne and I will increase your dose of Hannahpren. Problem solved."

"Until the next time." At the questioning look Seth shot me, I continued. "I guess you'll always know when to increase my medication. I start time traveling, and you better take it up a notch. At this rate, I'm going to have to be on a constant IV of the stuff before I'm 40. I wonder what the side effects of that will be. Will I grow a third arm?"

Seth squeezed my hand. "Don't worry, Hannah. You're not going to die or develop any new limbs. Wayne and I will figure it out."

I nodded silently. Seth and Wayne were probably among the top research doctors in the country. But I couldn't help but feeling like my life was once again strapped to a timer. If the Hannahpren had already stopped working as effectively, wouldn't the Karisenol as well? It seemed inevitable that eventually I would time travel and, when I returned, they wouldn't be able to stop the effects from killing me.

The searing pain in my temple was now too intense to ignore. *Just one foot in front of the other*, I told myself. We were almost to the hotel, now walking up the beach to the entrance. A wave of nausea hit. Blackness crept around the edges of my vision.

I felt my knees begin to buckle. I wasn't going to make it.

CHAPTER SIX

IN one smooth motion, Seth swept me back up into his arms, and began jogging to the hotel.

"Hang on, Hannah. We're almost there. You need to stay conscious."

I battled the blackness, dizziness, and nausea. If I lost control and drifted into unconsciousness, it would be more difficult for me to recover. I focused on the shadow of stubble on Seth's face. He hadn't shaved this morning, the slightly scruffy look making the strong planes of his face seem even more masculine and handsome.

As Seth ran through the lobby and boarded the elevator, I knew we had to be receiving some very curious looks, but I kept my focus on Seth's impassive face.

There was a ringing in my ears. I swallowed, trying to keep down the urge to be ill. As if from a distance, I heard Seth fumbling frantically with his key card while trying to keep me balanced in his arms.

I heard the soft beep as the door opened. Seth rushed inside and laid me on the bed. I heard his frantic movements, and before thirty seconds had passed, I felt the unmistakable prick of the injection.

"Hannah, are you still with me?

"Yes," I whispered. "Bucket."

A plastic waste basket magically appeared in front of me. Seth held me up while I had dry heaves, which was almost worse than having something on my stomach to throw up. Since it was afternoon now, and I hadn't eaten anything since dinner last night, the bucket's function was only for show.

I groaned in sheer misery, wanting to succumb to the numb blackness, but knowing I still needed to fight it. Mere seconds felt like hours. *It'll be better soon... It'll be better soon.* I kept repeating the mantra over and over in my mind.

Seth laid me back on the pillow and began strapping instruments to me, monitoring my vitals. Like water hitting parched ground, I felt the instant the medicine took effect. Gradually, the blackness receded, the pain lessened, and the nausea faded.

I opened my eyes to find Seth inspecting the instruments and taking my blood pressure.

Yes, my Prince Charming hadn't been fully honest with me, but he had also come on our honeymoon fully prepared to save my life and take care of me if necessary.

"Thank you," I whispered weakly, hoping the two little words would convey even a little of what I felt for my husband.

His gaze swung to mine. "You're going to be okay, Hannah. The medicine is doing its job. We have to give you injections at increasing intervals for the next few days, but you're over the worst now. This reaction wasn't as bad as others you've had. Probably because it's been over a year since your last time traveling episode."

"It wasn't as bad? It sure felt plenty bad to me. On the ten point pain scale, that was about a 15!"

"I'm sure it was, but at least you kept consciousness, which you haven't been able to do before. And your vital signs were never as erratic."

"Lucky me," I said sarcastically. "At least when I pass out, I get a little relief!"

I looked around at Seth's equipment attached to me and spread across the bed. "I didn't realize you'd come so prepared. I thought I was the one always concerned about the worst case scenario."

"Of course I came prepared. I don't take risks where you're concerned. You know I always take my medical bag wherever I go. I've just adapted it to ensure I have everything I may need to yet again save the life of my beautiful wife. You see, she's a bit of an adrenaline junky."

"Oh, yes. When I'm not time traveling, one of my favorite hobbies is jumping out of airplanes."

"Well, there was that one time that you thwarted a deadly mugging armed only with a flashlight."

"Yes, but it was a high voltage one," I shot back. "Seriously, though, don't you find it ironic that someone who's practically afraid of her own shadow and has to have her fingers pried out of the dash when someone else is driving is the one person on the planet who can time travel?"

Seth shrugged. "I don't pretend to understand God's

ways, but I do know He seems to have a pretty good sense of humor. I would say that His plans for you have turned out very well so far. We were able to save your mom and you were able to save me, all because of your time traveling. It seems like He's done well so far. I guess we just need to keep trusting Him in this latest hurdle."

I closed my eyes and tried to massage away the pain in my temples. Sometimes just thinking about the complicated mess God had obviously used for His purpose was enough to give me a headache. I still couldn't sort through or fathom all that had happened in my life.

Seeing my movements, Seth once again began checking his instruments. "Are you still in a lot of pain, Hannah? Maybe I should give you some pain meds as well."

"No, I think I'm fine at the moment. I'm just a bit light-headed, but I don't think it's anything food wouldn't cure. I haven't eaten anything since dinner last night."

"I'll order some room service. Why don't you try to get some rest while I get things packed."

"What do you mean 'packed'?" I asked suspiciously.

"I figure if you're feeling well enough, we could probably still catch a red eye flight back home tonight. I'll call Wayne so he'll be ready with some testing and a plan of action for your meds."

"No!" I said adamantly. "We are not cutting our honeymoon short, Seth McAllister! We just got here yesterday, and now we've wasted an entire day. We will have our honeymoon, and we will enjoy it, even if it kills us!"

"That's what I'm afraid of, Sweetheart! We need to get

you home to make sure you're okay and to adjust the Hannahpren so this doesn't happen again. You know, if you time travel again anytime soon, your chances of recovery diminish drastically."

"No, Seth." I felt my eyes fill with tears. "This trip is what I've dreamed of for so long. We'll only ever get one honeymoon. I'm fine now. You said you had enough Karisenol to get me through this. I'll just double my daily dose until you figure out the exact dosage."

The tears were now flowing in earnest, and I felt hiccuping sobs building up. My breath came in short gasps, and I started having trouble getting my words out. Alarmed, Seth immediately drew me into his arms, and began rubbing my back, trying to calm me down.

"Please, Seth. If our entire honeymoon is ruined…"

"Shhh, Hannah. Calm down. We won't go. It'll be okay. We'll stay and have a beautiful honeymoon."

I felt bad about freaking Seth out like that, but I couldn't help the panic that had overwhelmed me at his words. After several minutes, the tears and hiccuping finally slowed down enough for me to speak again.

"You promise? We can stay? You won't try to sedate me and get me on a plane back to San Francisco, will you?"

A slight twinkle of amusement lit his eyes. "No, Hannah. I promise. We'll do anything you want to do. I'll call Wayne, and will figure out a quick fix until we get home. It'll be okay. You just need to focus on staying calm and not getting upset. Please? I don't think *I* can handle you disappearing on me again."

I nodded shakily. "Okay," I said meekly.

Seth picked up the room service menu from the nightstand.

He was quiet.

I waited.

Wasn't he going to ask me what had happened? He'd said we were going to talk when we got to the hotel, but now he was showing an intense interest in the menu, and there was a strange tension between us. Seth had always been so open; I could talk to him about anything. He was normally a very outgoing, detail-oriented person, usually pestering me with more questions than I wanted to answer. I was the one who had to be coaxed out of my shell. But now, this strange, awkward silence was unnerving, and I didn't know how to deal with it.

So I feigned interest in the room's décor while he feigned interest in the menu. It was a beautiful room—the perfect honeymoon suite. It was done in an island theme, of course, with soft blues, greens, and tans. There was a sitting room area with a large, flat screen TV that could be easily viewed from the jetted tub, which, when the blinds were open, also looked out on the gorgeous ocean view. The bed sat at the back of the room with its satin bedspread mounted high with color-coordinated pillows. Opposite the tub was a small dining area. The monochromatic ocean color scheme was interrupted only by the lavish, fragrant bouquet of tropical flowers gracing the small table. My sweet Seth had ordered the flowers and arranged to have them waiting for me when we arrived yesterday.

This had to be one of the nicest rooms in the hotel. Natalie's room had been nice, but it hadn't been in the same league as this one. Seth had obviously spared no expense to make our honeymoon special.

Seth finally broke the silence. "It's almost dinner time anyway, so I'm going to order some food for myself as well. What sounds good to you?"

"You choose," I answered. "I'm so hungry that anything sounds good. I'll just have whatever you're having."

Seth continued to study the menu like it was one of his medical books.

Looking at the logo on the back, I asked, "Seth, why did you choose this hotel for our honeymoon?"

Seth looked up from the menu. "Natalie told me about it. I guess she stayed here when she came to Hawaii last year with Katherine. She said it was nice, and if Katherine hadn't been with her, she might have even considered it perfect."

The humor on Seth's face was chased away by a sudden shadow. "Why? Don't you like it?"

My heart melting at the sweet worry on his face, I hurried to explain. "Oh, yes. I love it! I just wondered because it seemed a little too much of a coincidence. When I went back, I saw Natalie. And Katherine."

"You saw Natalie? Here?" Seth paused, thoughtful. "So you went back a year? What—"

My cell phone rang from the nightstand beside us, interrupting his question. Seth picked it up.

"She's okay," Seth answered, obviously recognizing the number that had flashed on the screen. "Yes, we were right, but I found her in time, right after she returned."

He paused.

"No, I don't know any of the details yet."

He paused again. Then he extended the phone to me.

"It's your mom."

I flashed him an irate glare even as I accepted the phone. *You called my mom!* I mouthed angrily.

Seth only offered a shrug and an overly-innocent expression.

For the next few minutes, I answered my mom's worried questions as vaguely as possible while I watched Seth order room service and then use his cell phone to make a call to someone I assumed was Wayne. Seth had apparently told her I had time traveled again. If it had been up to me, I would have never told my parents. I knew they would now live in constant worry. As I already had to deal with that on a daily basis, I didn't like the idea of my parents feeling the same way.

I also didn't want to relive the whole experience for my mom, especially since I hadn't even had a chance to tell Seth about it. I basically just tried to reassure her that I was fine. Unfortunately, my mom wasn't satisfied with my answers and seemed determined to continue her interrogation until she got results.

"When did you travel to, Hannah? Did you change anything? Is everything okay?"

"Everything is fine. No, I didn't change anything. Look, Mom, can I please fill you in on the details when we get back? Seth is going to adjust my medication, so I'm going to recover fine and be perfectly safe. Now all I want to do is enjoy my honeymoon."

"Oh, of course, honey. I'm sorry. I wasn't thinking. I've just been so worried since Seth called wanting to know if we had heard from you. You and Seth go explore Hawaii. Take lots of pictures, and you can tell me all about your adventures when you get back. I love you. Your dad sends his love too."

"Thanks, Mom. I'll call you later to check in. Love you."

Seth was still on the phone with Wayne. Swinging my feet off the bed, I slowly stood, testing my strength. Thankfully, my legs were steady and the dizziness minimal.

It felt good to get cleaned up. A quick shower removed all the stowaway sand, and with a new change of clothes, I was soon feeling much better.

As I came out of the bathroom, there was a knock at the door. That was probably the room service. I opened the door to find the cart left for our convenience. I stepped out in the hall to push it inside. Suddenly, a door halfway down the long corridor slammed. A man stumbled out of a room followed by a woman who was screaming and hitting him with what looked to be some white, flimsy material.

Then I recognized the woman's weapon.

My negligée.

CHAPTER SEVEN

"I'M gone for one hour and you get busy with some trollop wearing this!" The ample woman was dressed in an overly-ample Hawaiian muumuu and was screaming while swinging the white bit of lace around the man's balding head. Interspersed with her attacks was a colorful assortment of names for her apparent husband and his supposed mistress.

Seth, hearing the commotion, finally hung up the phone and joined me in the hall. Doors opened up and down the hall as other hotel guests poked their heads out to gawk. But the feuding couple seemed oblivious to their audience.

"No!" The large man's colorful Hawaiian shirt was an exact match to his wife's dress. His long, handlebar mustache danced in the breeze as he simultaneously shook his head in frantic denial while dodging the flying negligée. For such a large man, he moved very quickly. "I went downstairs to talk to the guy at the front desk about one of those helicopter rides! I got back to the room five minutes before you did. Stop hitting me with that thing,

Woman!"

"You lie! You think someone snuck into our room and left this? Gary, this was supposed to be our second honeymoon!" The woman's anger was losing steam. She was still trying to flail the negligée, but she didn't have nearly the same accuracy with tears clouding her vision and streaming down her face.

I felt so helpless! The couple's room was the same one that had been Natalie's a year ago. I had no explanation for how my lingerie had ended up in their room. I had left it back with Natalie. But I couldn't just stand there and let a couple's marriage be torn apart because of me!

I looked at Seth in clear desperation. "It's mine!" I whispered fiercely.

By the look on his face, I knew he'd already recognized the offending object. He also seemed to understand my thoughts and intentions. He shook his head in a negative gesture, took my arm, and began urging me back in the room.

"There's nothing you can do, Hannah."

I resisted. "No, Seth. Please."

I looked up at him with pleading eyes. I knew he was afraid the scene would upset me. But not knowing what happened would be worse. My guilty conscience and my imagination would conspire to drive me crazier than the reality ever could.

I looked desperately back at the couple. What could I say? My mind flitted over the possibilities, but I came up with nothing. There was no reasonable explanation I could give to the couple as to how my negligée was in their room. The truth obviously wouldn't work, and none of the lies I could think of would even make sense.

So I watched helplessly as the heartbroken woman began sobbing, now using my negligée in the absence of a handkerchief.

I helplessly looked back up at Seth, desperate for a solution. If I went forward to claim my property, the woman would assume the worst, and I was pretty sure I wouldn't make it out without serious bodily injury.

"Maybe the maid left it!" Gary said, his voice still loud and echoing down the hall. "All I know is that I had nothing to do with it! I wasn't here! You can even go ask the guy at the front desk! We're supposed to be at the airport tomorrow morning at 9:00 for our helicopter tour."

"You scheduled it?" the woman sniffed. "I thought you said we couldn't afford it."

"This is our second honeymoon. We can afford it."

Sobs still shuddered through her body. And though slightly appeased, she still looked at her husband suspiciously.

"Please, Carla," the man said, his voice now quieter as he hesitantly reached out his hand to offer comfort. "Don't you know you're the only woman I'd want to see in a getup like that?"

Carla sniffed. "It wouldn't fit.

The man smiled and bravely leaned forward to whisper in her ear.

At his words, Carla ducked her head shyly, and I think

I even saw a slight rosy color fill her cheeks.

Gary and Carla then returned to their room, shutting the door softly behind them and seeming oblivious to the fact their epic battle had just provided entertainment for the entire fourth floor.

The drama concluded, all the spectators dismissed back to their own rooms. I held the door while Seth pushed the food cart inside.

The door shut, and I turned to Seth. "How did my lingerie end up in that room?"

Watching the spectacle had left me completely unnerved, and even now, though things seemed to have turned out alright, my hands still weren't quite steady.

Seth, seeming to ignore me, uncovered the food and placed it on the table.

I continued, "I left it in Natalie's room, but that was a year ago! There's no way it could have stayed there for a year and then just now been discovered. It's too much of a coincidence."

Seth sat down and began eating, still annoyingly calm in the face of my crisis.

"Was Gary and Carla's room the same one Natalie was staying in a year ago?" he finally asked.

"Yes. At least I think so. I didn't see the room number."

"Remember the first time you time traveled, Hannah? You took your SUV with you. When I woke the next morning, I found you missing, but your SUV was gone too. When you traveled back to your original time, your vehicle traveled with you, even though you weren't in it."

I felt more than a little stupid. Why hadn't I ever thought about this before? How had my SUV made it back?

"I guess you've given this some thought," I mused. "I thought only things I was directly touching traveled with me, like my clothes, or like when you traveled with me."

"That's true when you travel from your initial time, but somehow you seem to leave some kind of marker on everything you take with you, like a time stamp. When you return, everything else returns to its original time as well, whether or not you're in close proximity."

As I tried to wrap my mind around this new realization, my agitation was momentarily distracted, and I rather unconsciously joined Seth at the table and began eating.

"And what is your scientific explanation for this? It almost sounds like magic."

Seth shrugged. "I have no explanation. But it's not as if time travel is a science or we have any sort of documented data. You and your experiences are all we have. And although Wayne would love the opportunity to do every kind of time travel experiment imaginable, we know that's not possible. All we can do is make observations based on your limited experiences."

I was so absorbed, I barely noticed that my steak was excellent. Seth had ordered mahi mahi for himself, but since I wasn't a fan of fish, he had chosen a New York strip steak for me. I lost track of how many rolls I ate, and the baked potato, fresh fruit, and pie seemed to disappear as well.

As my thoughts played chase in my brain, I mused aloud. "So when I came back at the beach, my negligée must have suddenly appeared in that room; only it wasn't Natalie's room anymore. I can't believe I never thought about how my SUV got back that very first time!"

"Don't feel bad. It took me a while to realize it as well. I knew the things you were in direct contact with traveled with you, I just didn't think about the return trip until Wayne and I were discussing it one day."

"And you didn't think to mention it to me?"

Seth shrugged. "I didn't think it necessary. You weren't supposed to time travel again. And you definitely weren't supposed to time travel in a sexy teddy."

As a blush crept into my cheeks, Seth apparently saw the humor in the whole situation and started laughing. A mental picture of poor Carla finding my lingerie in her bedroom sent me into peals of laughter as well. Then my mind jumped to replay the scene where she was hitting Gary with the slinky garment. Tears streamed down my face, and I felt I couldn't catch my breath from laughing so hard. Every time I would start to get control, I would look at Seth, and we would both break out in another fit of hilarity.

Unfortunately, all the laughing only made the pain in my head worse.

Noticing the soft 'ow's' interspersed with my giggles as I held my head, Seth seemed to sober-up quickly. "Come on, it's time for your next dose."

After the food and injection, I suddenly became very sleepy. Wanting to get more comfortable, I brushed my teeth and got ready for bed, intending to then talk to Seth about what had happened. But as I lay on the bed, watching Seth put his medical kit back together, I couldn't seem to form any coherent thoughts. And Seth didn't ask. Why didn't he ask?

"HANNAH, are you upset with me?" Seth asked as he followed me up the trail.

No, I was not 'upset' with him; I was hurt.

I didn't turn around, but kept my fast pace on the narrow, winding trail. "Upset? What makes you think I'm upset?"

We were on a hike to what was supposed to be a fabulous waterfall. If he wasn't smart enough to figure out why I was "upset," then I certainly wasn't going to tell him. It should be obvious. I was on my honeymoon with my gorgeous husband, and he was acting as if I had the plague.

When I woke this morning, he was already out of bed with a list of sites to see and activities to do for the day. While I certainly didn't mind a busy schedule, I did mind that my new husband hadn't kissed me since we were on the beach yesterday. The only time he'd touched me was when administering my injections. The fun, playful attitude that had marked our first day as husband and wife was gone, replaced by a strange awkwardness. I could never recall feeling awkward around Seth, but it almost seemed as if he wouldn't look me in the eye.

It also bothered me that he hadn't yet asked me about

what had happened when I went back in time. On the beach he'd said we'd talk about it later, but he'd never again mentioned it, instead keeping to small talk about points of interest on the island.

Something was bothering him. I'd tried to be patient. But what if he'd decided marrying me was a mistake? We'd thought I wouldn't time travel again. Knowing that his wife could disappear at any time might be a deal breaker for him.

Deep down, I knew Seth loved me, and I tried to hold onto the anger instead of the fear. If I was angry with him, maybe I wouldn't have to face the terror of the thought that he didn't want me anymore.

Seth remained silent, not answering my barbed question, but choosing to follow me at my reckless pace.

It was about a mile long hike, and we didn't see many other tourists. This hike wasn't one of the most popular, so we only passed a few other couples coming down the trail. The utter silence of the rainforest around me should have been soothing. The only sound was my rapid breathing. Even our footsteps were muffled by the thick carpet of earth and foliage that made up the narrow trail. Everything around me was a deep green. Huge leaves and ferns stood in attendance alongside the trail while trees draped their finery overhead.

I should have been awed by the beautiful setting, the fresh scent of wet growing earth, and the aura of peace it created. Instead, I was marching up the trail as if on a mission while alternating between rehearsing tirades in my head and feeling hot tears burn the back of my eyes.

I came upon the waterfall suddenly, barging through to

a clearing where crystal-clear water cascaded like a bridal veil into a calm pool below. The tranquility of the place hit me as if it was a physical force, and I immediately stopped. I felt somehow as if I was intruding on holy ground, like entering a church on Sunday when you were so mad you couldn't see straight. My feelings stood in stark contrast to this sanctuary. I stood still, closed my eyes, and breathed deeply, feeling my tension submit to the overwhelming peace.

I felt Seth come up from behind and gently enfold me in his embrace.

"Hannah, what's wrong? Why are you mad at me?"

The serenity of this place still couldn't stop my tears. Brokenly, I whispered, "Seth, do you regret marrying me?"

I felt Seth's entire body startle at my question. Turning me around to face him, he put his finger to my chin, forcing me to look him in the eye.

"Never," he replied adamantly. "I'm crazy in love with you Hannah. Don't you know that? The best day of my life was the day before yesterday, when I married you. Why would you ask such a thing?"

"You haven't touched or kissed me since yesterday. You haven't even asked me about what happened when I time traveled. We're on our honeymoon, and I feel like you want nothing to do with me!"

Seth groaned. "Oh, Hannah! I'm sorry. I should have said something sooner. I've just been too afraid of your answers." Seth closed his eyes briefly, as if trying to psych himself up for an unpleasant task. Then he reopened them, a light of determination now in his gaze. "Do you regret marrying me?"

I just stared at him, eyes wide in shock. "Are you kidding me?"

"I need to know, Hannah. Did I do something to upset you? If I did, just tell me, and we can work it out. I woke yesterday morning to find you gone, and I've been miserable ever since. What did I do? What upset you so much to make you time travel?"

Everything suddenly clicked into place, and I understood. Every other time I'd time traveled had been triggered by my extreme emotions, mostly fear and anger, or a combination of the two. My sweet husband had been blaming himself, feeling afraid that he had done something to upset me so bad that I had time traveled. Now he was scared to find out what he had done and scared to do anything that might upset me again and inadvertently trigger more time travel.

"Seth, you didn't do anything wrong! I wasn't upset at all. I was… happy!"

Seth looked confused. "You weren't upset? You think you time traveled because you were happy?"

"I was on my honeymoon in Hawaii after having the wedding of my dreams! I woke up with my wonderful, gorgeous, amazing husband beside me. I got up and snuck out to the balcony to see the sunrise, and I felt happier than I ever remember feeling in my entire life. You make me so unbelievably happy, Seth."

I watched the play of emotions across his face. At first, he seemed very relieved to find out it wasn't his fault. But then, as my words sank in, I watched as a new fear dawned in his eyes. The second the realization hit, I felt him emotionally withdraw from me, and he looked away.

I knew exactly what he was thinking.

"No, Seth, look at me. You can't do this to me! Please! Don't stop loving me! You can't live in fear that you might make me too upset, too angry, or too *happy*! It'll completely destroy me if you try! It doesn't work to try to shield me from emotions, remember? It only makes things worse."

When it didn't seem like my words were sinking in, I continued. "You're the one who's always telling me that God is the one in control. I can't stop living. If I time travel tomorrow because you made me unbelievably happy, it will have been worth it, even if it doesn't end well. I want to live to the fullest every moment I have left with you. I want to feel every emotion. Please, Seth. Don't hold back. Love me."

Seth's expression was intense as he stepped forward suddenly and pulled me into his embrace. He kissed me deeply, thoroughly, passionately, as if it might be our last kiss in forever. All his pent-up emotions were channeled into that one expression. I knew he was still afraid. All his fear, worry, and love were put into his kiss. I didn't know if I'd ever breathe again, and I wasn't sure I wanted to.

I propped myself up with my elbow and looked down at Seth lying in bed beside me. His eyes were closed, but I knew he wasn't asleep. We had spent the evening back at our hotel, ordering room service while Seth did his best to make me very happy.

I had planned on telling Seth everything about my trip

back a year. I had wanted to thoroughly interrogate him and find out exactly why a group of men wanted my husband dead. I wanted to know for sure if the mugging really had been 'random.' I needed to know how much Seth truly knew about the situation. Had he known he was targeted? Had he simply let me believe it had been a random mugging?

As I watched the rise and fall of his muscular chest, I suddenly felt unsure about my previous plans.

Maybe I shouldn't tell him what I'd overheard.

It had been a year since the meeting I had witnessed. Maybe Katherine had handled it as she'd said. Maybe the danger was past. Maybe the mugging had been a coincidence. There certainly hadn't been any other threatening situations since then.

"Seth, what are you working on?" I asked thoughtfully.

"Right now, I'm working on studying the inside of my eyelids," Seth replied dryly.

Ignoring his attempt at humor, I clarified. "No, I mean at work. What projects are you working on?"

Seth groaned, still not bothering to open his eyes. "Hannah, you know exactly what I'm working on. You file the papers for all the projects. We have about a dozen different ones going on right now. Everything from special cancer cases to the water analysis of an area."

Seth was right. I did do a lot of the paperwork for the Tomorrow Foundation. Even though I was in a Master's program for Chemistry, I still managed to put in hours to help Seth and Wayne. It was also very convenient that some of my studies and internships could be completed right there with the Foundation.

But I wouldn't think any of the current projects I'd seen would be enough to get Seth killed. They were all fairly standard, with no dramatic findings.

I needed to figure out what it was that had put his life in danger. Maybe then I could know if he was now safe.

"But are you working on anything controversial?"

Seth's eyes popped open and he turned on his side to look at me. I knew I had gone a bit too far with that question.

"What do you mean 'controversial?' What's up with the questions, Hannah? Did something happen when you went back in time? Did you change history in some way?"

I tried not to panic. Seth was too smart. I couldn't play twenty questions with him and have him not be suspicious. I either needed to confess everything or figure a way out of this very quickly.

"No, I didn't change history. I didn't have the chance to do much damage to the timeline. I was too busy running all over the hotel in my negligée, trying not to get arrested."

Seth's eyes widened, and an ornery glint of humor shown in their blue-green depths. "Hmm… you running around the hotel in a negligée. Would you care to reenact it so I can fully understand what happened?"

And Seth's attention was successfully diverted.

I playfully swatted him with a pillow. "No, thank you! That's definitely not an experience I'd ever want to repeat! Now that I think about it though, I might have changed history for the poor couple who was staying in this same room a year ago! They were more than a little disturbed when I walked in on them in bed!"

At Seth's urging, I launched into retelling my experience. Fortunately, I had already begun to see a little humor in the whole idea of time traveling in my lingerie and then having to sneak through the hotel to locate some clothes. Somewhere between me telling how I interrupted the other couple in what I'd thought was my room and me describing how I hid in the cleaning closet, Seth began practically rolling with laughter. It only got worse as I told the story of sneaking down the stairs and then trying to get into the women's changing room. I gave a dramatic retelling, never letting on that I was omitting anything. I just skipped the entire part about overhearing Katherine's meeting. In fact, I didn't mention Katherine at all.

"So what did Natalie say when you told her that you'd time traveled?" Seth asked. "Did she unleash an entire stream of British slang?"

I paused, momentarily stumped. How was I going to explain and not return the conversation to a more serious note and the inevitable questions about Katherine?

"I didn't tell her," I said, trying to keep it simple. "She didn't want to know. I shrugged. "You know, Natalie. She's a difficult one to understand. I tried to tell her, but she wouldn't let me. She just wanted to help without knowing why. She's witnessed more than enough strange things about me over the years, but she's never wanted to know. But I did hear plenty of British terms when she was trying to get me from the pool up to her room. Do you have any idea what a bolt-hole is?"

And once again, I'd steered Seth onto safe ground.

Waves of guilt lapped at my conscience. I fully understood that I was doing a stellar job of manipulating the conversation and deceiving Seth. I'd never thought of myself as manipulative and deceitful. I'd always tried to be honest and live with integrity. But the safety of the man I loved had never depended on my knowledge.

Nothing had happened since the mugging almost a year ago. I knew if I mentioned what I'd overheard, Seth wouldn't let it go. He would question Katherine, dig up any old research he could find, and leave not a stone unturned until he had all the information and brought people to justice. It was very possible that he'd stumbled on research that he hadn't even realized was significant. I knew what he was working on now, and nothing sounded remotely like what they had been discussing in the meeting.

I hated the thought of trusting Katherine, but maybe I should. She had seemed confident that she would take care of the situation and protect Seth. She had obviously done that now for a year. I could make things worse by interfering. Seth may not be in danger now, but I knew without a doubt, he would be if I told him.

So I determinedly ignored my conscience and the guilt that accused me. I smiled as if I didn't have a care and leaned over to meet his lips with mine.

I had been married three days, and I was already working very hard to keep a secret from my husband.

CHAPTER EIGHT

Six months later

IT was just an ordinary piece of paper. I had already sorted probably hundreds just like it. It looked just like one of the many pages of project notes Seth and Wayne kept for every project they worked on. But the second I skimmed the words on the page, I knew this one was different. My heart started pounding, and I quickly plopped down in the desk chair.

This was what I had been alternately searching for and dreading for the past few months. After finding no leads, I had finally almost persuaded myself that it had never existed to begin with. Now I held the proof in my hand, and I had the awful urge to burn it and rush back to the lovely denial of mere seconds before.

Without a doubt, I instantly knew this was the research that had almost gotten Seth killed.

To the casual observer, the paper didn't look threatening at all. It was just another standard page of notes in the same format Seth and Wayne used to document all of their projects. They were both meticulous about documenting everything, but they were lousy at organizing it.

I usually followed behind them and made their work functional and accessible. Because of my background in science, I could decipher their notes and transplant them to the correct file. While the two doctors fully intended to involve me in the projects more directly after I graduated with my Master's degree in May, I wasn't sure who would clean up after them if I was otherwise occupied.

With my finals coming up, I'd needed to get ahead at the office so I could focus on studying. I had arrived at the office this morning determined to tame the chaos. I had already cleared off my desk and had now moved on to Seth's. He and Wayne were usually good about making sure important documents made it into my inbox. I typically stayed away from their own personal desks, figuring they should at least clean up their own mess. But, thinking I'd surprise my husband with a clean work area when he returned from his meeting, I'd enthusiastically invaded his space and tackled the task.

Now my hand shook as I held the dreaded document. It was dated eighteen months ago, exactly around the time of the meeting I had witnessed in Hawaii. Frantically, I searched through the pile on his desk, looking for other papers that matched this one. I found two more, but none with a more recent date. I felt a twinge of relief. Maybe this was just an old project that he'd stopped over a year ago and had no intention of continuing.

Besides the date, the fact that I had never before seen notes on this project was enough to make me fear the worst. I forced myself to quiet my racing thoughts and focus on understanding exactly what I was looking at. I felt almost sick as I read. Unfortunately, I was able to decipher all of the project details and their potentially deadly significance.

The papers I was holding covered the overview of the project and some of Seth's notes. There was apparently much more of the actual research somewhere else. From what I could tell, Seth and Wayne had been studying antidepressant medications. During their research, they had unexpectedly found that certain medications seemed to cause an increased dependency that required increasing medication to satisfy. But the most alarming finding was the potential side effects to the body if that increased dependency wasn't met. The result could be essentially fatal withdrawals if the medication was not increased in correlation with the increasing dependence.

In other words, if a patient taking this medication tried to stop, or even kept their same dosage for too long, they could face serious damage to their body and possibly even die.

No wonder they had wanted to kill Seth! If the company who made the drug had known about the problem and failed to notify or do anything about it, this research could destroy them, showing them to be potentially responsible for many serious health problems and deaths.

However, there was a problem with the research. Seth and Wayne had no evidence. Everything I could find was conjecture mostly based on their analysis of the chemical composition of the drug. I could find no record of any studies or testing they had done to confirm their speculation.

I began a thorough search of Seth's entire desk. I sorted every scrap of paper, opened every drawer, and even bent down underneath to check for any secret compartments. If they had finished their research and found concrete evidence, then none of Katherine's good intentions would be able to save Seth.

While looking at the underside of the desk, my cell phone rang. Without even glancing at the incoming number, I answered it.

"Hello?"

"Hi, Hannah." Natalie's British accent was immediately recognizable. "Are we still on for this weekend?"

"This weekend?" I asked, distractedly.

"Yes. We're supposed to go Christmas shopping together. You're going to help me pick out a fabulous dress for my office Christmas party. Remember?"

"Oh, okay. Sure. That should be fine. Why don't you just text me the time and place?"

There was a pause on the other end.

"Hannah, is everything okay? You sound a little upset."

I closed my eyes, trying to fight the burning behind my eyes. "It's not something I can talk to you about, Natalie."

By the silence on the other end, I knew Natalie had understood my meaning.

"How is your mom, doing?" I asked quietly.

"She seems to be doing fine. She has some testing next month to see if they got all of the cancer." Natalie was subdued, which was a rarity.

"Let me know how it goes. And let me know if and when your dad is ever able to retire."

"You'll be my first call," Natalie said. "I guess I'll see you on Saturday. I'll let you know what time."

Yet Natalie didn't hang up.

After the space of a few seconds, she continued. "Hannah, you know I don't like leaving you on your tod when you're upset."

"I'll be okay," I said, deliberately trying to brighten my tone. "I certainly didn't mean to stress you to the point that your British colors start showing and you begin using phrases I can't hope to understand. Better be careful, Natalie. Any more stress and you'll be 'having kittens'!"

Natalie laughed at my attempt at using one of her phrases. At least she was a good sport about being teased. She was aware of her tendency to revert when upset or stressed, and sometimes I think she threw in a few special colloquialisms just for my benefit.

Even though Natalie had accepted my diversion and soon signed off, I could tell she was still bothered. She didn't like not knowing what was wrong, and she really didn't like not being able to help me.

When Seth and I had returned from our honeymoon, I had been anxious to see Natalie. Unable to wait until she got off work, I'd gone to her office, hoping to catch her on her lunch break. She'd been in a meeting when I'd arrived. I'd walked by the windows fronting the conference room, thinking to wait on one of the couches in the reception area. Natalie had looked up as I passed. Catching her eye, I had smiled and lifted up the shirt and shorts I had borrowed from her on my time diversion in Hawaii.

Natalie's eyes flew wide and I saw her mouth a word I was sure was not quite appropriate for her meeting. Shocked, I quickly found a couch, not wanting to distract my friend any more.

Less than thirty seconds later, Natalie emerged from the conference room, grabbed my arm, and pulled me down the hall to her small office. After shutting the door firmly, she turned to me.

But I spoke first. "Natalie, I didn't mean to ruin your meeting. I can wait."

Natalie waved off my concern with impatience. "Forget it, Hannah. It wasn't an official meeting. It was just an informal lunch to discuss the on-call schedule for over the holidays. You can't wave those clothes like a flag and expect me to not come running."

A tense silence stretched between us as we stared at each other. There was so much to say. Natalie hadn't ever mentioned anything about the Hawaii trip that was, for her, a year ago. For me, the entire experience was so fresh. I remembered the lengths she'd gone to help me, yet she'd asked me to reveal nothing.

Now I was free to tell her everything. I opened my mouth to speak.

Natalie held up her hand. "No, Hannah, don't tell me."

Natalie was normally such a vivacious person. The misery on her face was something I hadn't seen before.

"My mom has cancer," she said quietly.

I was stunned into silence. Why hadn't she mentioned this before? I was her friend. I would have wanted to help and support her from the very beginning.

Natalie sighed. "When she was diagnosed several months ago, my dad had to make the decision to postpone retirement. They need the medical insurance and benefits he gets with his job."

I searched Natalie's eyes, and I understood what she was saying. She was not free.

"Thank you for returning my clothes, Hannah," she said rather formally, as if reciting the lines of a play. "I'd just about given up on you ever giving them back."

"You had to have known, Natalie," I whispered, feeling as if I were entering into a forbidden conversation. "You were the one who suggested Hawaii to Seth. You knew that's where we were going on our honeymoon."

A slightly bemused expression lit her face, and her white teeth flashed in a quick grin. "Well, yes. I might have seen some ulterior reason for suggesting Hawaii to Seth. But I have had an awful lot of time to think about it. You had said to wait until you yourself mentioned something. You hadn't even hinted at it yet, and I guess I was getting a little impatient to get my clothes back."

I'd already known that Natalie was brilliant, so it shouldn't have come as a shock that she understood much more than she would ever admit.

"Theories, Natalie?" I asked quietly, watching her face.

As if slamming a door, Natalie's expression suddenly closed as an impassive mask had once again slipped into place. "Thanks again for returning my clothes, Hannah."

"Hannah, why are you sitting under Seth's desk?" Wayne's voice startled me back to the present. I jerked, dropping the cell phone I'd been staring at blindly, lost in the memory.

I crawled out from under the desk and stood. "It never hurts to practice for earthquakes," I answered flippantly, trying to hide my embarrassment. Looking at the papers spread across the desk, I resorted to honesty—sort of. "Wayne, I'm trying to get Seth's desk organized, but I'm not sure what to do with these notes. They look like they're probably from a larger file, but I don't recognize the project."

I carefully watched Wayne's face as he took one of the papers. His eyes widened briefly, but he quickly covered his reaction. "I can take care of them for you. They belong to an old project, but since we never got anywhere with it, Seth probably just intends to shred the whole thing."

Wayne gathered the papers, and I didn't question him further, choosing to let him believe I didn't understand exactly what the project was about. I had seen his reaction, however brief. This was not just an old project; it was far more important. Wayne knew that. He had immediately recognized it but was trying to throw me off track with his nonchalant attitude.

"Was there something you needed, Wayne?" I asked. When Seth and Wayne had originally started the Tomorrow Foundation, Wayne would frequently take breaks from his work to visit or joke with me. He had always been Seth's best friend, but he was also a wonderful friend to me.

Over time, though, Wayne had taken fewer visiting breaks, and now, when I was in the office, I rarely saw him. He was perpetually busy, never stopping his work.

I had always appreciated that Wayne wasn't your typical genius. He actually had a life, interests, and personality outside his gifted field. Now, though, I had noticed him devoting more and more of himself to the Foundation, and it made me sad. He was way too busy, and I hated to see him sacrifice so much of himself. Him showing up and speaking to me was actually an unusual occurrence.

"I was wondering if you knew when Seth was supposed to be back. There are a few things I need to go over with him."

"He said he was going to be back this afternoon. I think his meeting extends through lunch. He was planning to return after that."

Wayne nodded, and an awkward, strangely tense silence stretched between us. I didn't understand it. When had I ever felt awkward around Wayne? Confused, I searched for a topic, any subject that would chase away the tension.

But Wayne spoke before I could come up with anything. "Well, I guess I'll go grab myself some lunch. I can't go any further in my current project without Seth's input. Can I bring something back for you?"

It struck me as a bit curious that he offered to 'bring something back,' but he didn't ask me to go with him. We used to go to lunch together all the time.

"No, thanks," I said. "I'm supposed to meet my sister, Abby, for lunch. She's in the city for some shopping and wanted to get together." I glanced at the clock. "In fact, I should be leaving right now."

Wayne left with the project notes firmly in hand. I put

the last finishing touches on Seth's desk, grabbed my purse, and left to meet Abby. She was already waiting at a table when I arrived. It had become somewhat of a tradition for us to meet at this place. The food was good, but we really came for the cheesecake.

We quickly placed our usual orders and started talking. I soon realized though that I had no idea what Abby had been talking about. I was so preoccupied with Seth and the project notes that I couldn't seem to get my mind to focus on my sister.

I sat up straighter and tried to forcibly focus on what she was saying. I didn't want to ever have the guilt of not being there for her. I tried to keep my part of the conversation light and supportive, not wanting her to know there was anything wrong. I couldn't add my problems to hers; she had enough to handle already.

Abby was normally a very happy, open person, but over the past eighteen months or so, I'd watched her fade like a flower. Her eyes no longer sparkled; her smile was noticeably absent. Even her normally bouncy blond hair seemed to hang limp, as if she wasn't putting as much effort into her appearance. She tried to put on a good front, especially in front of our parents, but I knew something was very wrong in her life.

But Abby wouldn't talk about it. Early on, I had dropped deliberate hints, trying to get her to talk. When that hadn't been successful, I had asked her outright what was going on. She had refused to answer, saying that nothing was wrong. We had finally gotten in a big fight, with Abby saying her life was none of my business. She'd pretty much told me to butt out, and if I needed to know something, she'd tell me.

It was extremely hurtful to see the dark circles under Abby's eyes and the obvious pain in her expression, but it was even more hurtful that she wouldn't share what was going on. We had always been close—best friends. But I loved her enough to back off. When she was ready to talk, I'd be there. And if she never talked to me and her life finally crumbled, I would be there to pick up the pieces.

Of course, I had my suspicions of what was troubling her. It was her marriage. It broke my heart to think that Tom and Abby, once so much in love, were now causing each other such pain. When Abby had first met and married Tom, I'd had some misgivings, but Abby had been head-over-heels in love. I liked Tom, but he was very much opposite Abby in personality. Even more troubling was that, though he claimed to be a Christian, I worried he was a Christian more for Abby's sake than due to a genuine commitment.

They had been such happy newlyweds, but things seemed to go downhill after they'd bought Silver Springs. I knew they had made the decision together, but after moving and taking over the business, it soon became clear that Tom hated it. Tom wasn't a social butterfly like Abby, and he didn't enjoy having to interact with guests. He was a computer geek who felt much more at home in front of a computer screen than he did doing the outdoor maintenance Silver Springs management required. Added to all that, he seemed to hate the isolation of the mountains.

I also suspected Abby wanted a baby. And I couldn't imagine Tom feeling the same way. He hadn't ever struck me as the paternal type.

Although I had my theories, I didn't have any real insider knowledge of their relationship. I knew my mom had attempted to talk to Abby as well, but as far as I knew, she hadn't gotten any further than I had. What most disturbed me was that it wasn't like Abby to clam up so much. I didn't think there was anything as bad as abuse going on in their relationship, but I really didn't know exactly what was happening.

The end result was that I continued to be there for Abby as much as I could, enduring superficial conversations and feeling the helpless frustration of watching my sister's depression, all in hopes of being there when she finally realized she needed me.

With Abby's problems and now my own, it was no wonder I was developing a nasty headache. What was I going to do about Seth? Should I confront him about the project? Should I admit the secret I'd been keeping from him since our honeymoon?

"Okay, Hannah, spill it. What's wrong?" My focus swerved back to Abby sitting across from me.

"What are you talking about?" I asked, feigning confusion.

"You're not listening to a word I'm saying. You haven't been paying attention to me since you got here. So what's bothering you?"

"I'm sorry, Abby. You were saying something about an idea you had for Mom and Dad for Christmas, right?"

"Nice try, Hannah, but I can read you like a book. I always know when something's bothering you. And you're wearing worry like makeup today."

Abby wasn't nearly as good at reading me as she liked to think. She wasn't the only one who had secrets she wasn't willing to share. Abby found out about my time traveling and the resulting health problems when they initially began, but she was now under the impression that both were completely under control. She also knew nothing about the fact that I wasn't technically her sister.

And I had no intention of telling her.

My parents and I had agreed that it wasn't something that she needed to know right now. The fact that we weren't blood sisters in no way changed how I felt about her. She was my sister in every way that mattered.

Besides, she had enough on her plate as it was. She herself had been so preoccupied that she hadn't really questioned all the bizarre circumstances surrounding me, which in itself was unusual for her. Normal Abby wouldn't rest until she had ferreted out every last detail of my life.

So, no, I was not going to spill my guts to Abby. It did, however, irk me that she was asking me to share my troubles when she wasn't willing to do the same. Even more irksome was the knowledge that I would need to tell her some version of the truth to get her to back off.

"You're right, Abby. I'm sorry I'm not very good company today. I'm afraid I've really screwed things up with Seth. There's something I should have told him months ago, but I didn't because I thought I was protecting him. Now I'm afraid if I tell him, he'll be very angry and the situation will be that much worse. Have you ever kept something from Tom?"

Intrinsic in my confession was the small hope that maybe, if I spoke with honesty about my marriage, she would follow suit.

Abby was silent as the waitress placed a piece of cheesecake in front of each of us. As usual, we had split an entrée so as to be sure we would have room for what we really wanted for lunch.

To Abby's credit, she didn't ask what my secret was or the details of my problems with Seth.

"I'm the last person you should ask for marriage advice, Hannah. I think I'm probably the opposite of an expert."

I was surprised. That was the closest Abby had ever come to admitting she and Tom were having issues.

"But I do know you need to be completely honest with Seth," she continued. Secrets will kill your trust and your relationship. They are like poison. Seth loves you. It might take some work, but if you're honest, he'll forgive you. The longer you let it go, the worse it will be. If you wait too long, it might be too late."

"It's not too late for you, is it, Abby?" I asked gently. I didn't want to put too much pressure on her, but this was the first hint she'd ever given.

Abby made a face, as if she'd gotten a whiff of something rotten. "I certainly hope not. But you can't exactly be married alone. My feelings aren't the only ones that matter."

"Maybe things will improve after mom and dad move up there," I said, trying to offer encouragement. "At least they can take off a little of the pressure and workload. Don't you think that will make things better for you and Tom?"

Abby sighed. "We've been waiting for Mom and Dad to move for almost a year now. It took so much longer than we thought for that company to get the permits and everything approved for the purchase of the property. Now

Mom and Dad are finally moving to Silver Springs next month, and I can't wait! I know the dead of winter is the worst possible time to move in the Sierras, but it will be such a relief to have them. I think I'll lose it if they are delayed even a day!

"Things are in pretty bad shape, then?"

Abby nodded. "There are a lot of repairs that need to be done. I've been so overwhelmed; I haven't even bothered with much advertising and marketing lately. We have very few guests scheduled in December and none at all around the holidays. I haven't even used the outer cabins since the end of August. If I can just get some help, we'll be able to get back on our feet and start making a profit again."

I was well-aware Abby had steered the conversation away from her personal life and back onto the safe ground of her business. I also knew it would be pointless to try to redirect the conversation or ask her pointed questions.

I would have to be satisfied for now with the tidbits of information she had already revealed. Yes, she and Tom were having serious problems, and at this point, it seemed terribly clear that Abby was worried her marriage might be a lost cause.

Abby's words and the look on her face stayed with me long after Abby and I had hugged goodbye and went our separate ways. I prayed for Abby's marriage, but I prayed even more fervently for my own.

If I waited to tell Seth the truth, it might be too late on more than one level. He might not forgive me, but he also might stumble into being the target of dangerous people determined to keep him from exposing *their* secret.

But if I told him now, he still might not forgive me, and it might make him even more determined to charge straight toward the enemy. There was no way I could win. I either faced losing my marriage or losing the man I loved. Suddenly I felt as if I was being strangled by the secret I'd spent the last six months trying to forget.

CHAPTER NINE

I groaned and tossed my pen on the desk. I had reread the same page about four times and still couldn't recall a single fact from it. I rubbed my eyes. It was useless to try to continue studying when my mind was so preoccupied.

I knew what I had to do. This wasn't going to get any easier. If I had any hope of passing my upcoming finals, I needed to relieve the pressure and tell Seth the truth.

My stomach did flip flops as I stood, but I didn't give myself the chance to second-guess and change my mind. Abby's words from earlier in the day still echoed in my mind, and I knew that if I had any hope of being able to study, or even sleep, in the near future, I needed a clean conscience and an assurance from Seth that everything truly was okay.

Leaving our bedroom, I found Seth in the living room playing his guitar. We had chosen to live in a small apartment close to the university. We were hoping to later purchase a house, but until the Tomorrow Foundation was fully established and secure, we had wanted to focus on saving our money.

Some aspects of apartment living had been a difficult adjustment. Seth's favorite form of relaxation was to play his guitar, which wasn't necessarily appreciated at all hours of the night by our neighbors. Seth had accordingly adapted to play very quietly.

I could only hope that he was sufficiently relaxed to extend me forgiveness and understanding when he found out my secret.

I sat on the floor directly in front of where Seth sat on the couch. I looked him in the eyes and spoke without preamble, just launching in and hoping for possibly a little shock effect. "Seth, when I cleaned up your desk today, I found some notes on a project I knew nothing about."

I had full intention of telling him everything on my end, but I still had the unshakable feeling that he himself had secrets. So I carefully watched his reaction, hoping it would tell me what I needed to know.

His eyes flashed, but were soon covered by a wary, guarded look, as if this was almost an expected conversation. And that's when I knew. Wayne had already told him I'd found the papers. He'd been warned. I should have expected as much; Wayne always told Seth everything.

"You mean the research on the antidepressants?" he asked. "That was just an old project from before you started working with us. It was before we officially started the Tomorrow Foundation. We actually started it because we were searching for some medication to help you. But the research never went anywhere, and then you got a much better alternative from your mom's research. We haven't worked on that project in well over a year. I was going through some old files, which is why the notes were on the desk."

"And how long did it take you and Wayne to come up with that cover story?" I asked quietly.

Seth was silent. We stared at each other. My gaze was challenging. His was almost assessing—as if he was trying to figure out exactly how much I knew.

Finally, he spoke. "Hannah, I'm not sure what you think you know, but I told you the truth."

"But is it the whole truth?" I shot back.

"I don't understand. Why are you even questioning me about this? It's just an old project that dead-ended."

"It is not 'just an old project!' You and I both know it is much more than that! I read the notes, Seth! I *understood* the notes! Having research that shows a very popular antidepressant is harmful and potentially fatal is dangerous. What if someone doesn't want the information to get out?"

"Is that what you're worried about? Hannah, I'm telling you, I haven't worked on the thing in almost a year and a half. It went nowhere. Yes, I had my suspicions, but if you read the notes, you should know I had no proof. I never got any proof. Nobody knew about that research, and without evidence, that project is about as threatening as your sweet grandmother."

"You're wrong. People did know about your research. And it was dangerous enough to try to have you killed!"

"Hannah, what are you talking about?" Seth asked with an almost-exaggerated calm, though he did seem to pale slightly under his healthy tan.

My gaze faltered. "When we were in Hawaii and I

went back in time, I overheard a meeting between Katherine and some of her clients. Seth, you're right. The medication is dangerous. But the company already knows about it and is trying to cover it up. They knew what you were working on and were planning to stop you by using whatever means necessary. They had to have been behind the mugging. Seth, they were trying to have you killed!"

"And you didn't tell me this sooner, Hannah? Why not?"

"I was trying to protect you!" I said miserably, but I couldn't meet his eyes. I'd never seen him so angry. And it was directed at me.

I rushed to explain. "In the meeting, Katherine had assured them that she would take care of the problem and stop you without the drastic measures they were discussing. She was also going to find a way to falsify records and effectively cover up the truth so they would appear innocent if the dangerous side effects were ever discovered. That was a year and a half ago. I'm sure the mugging was an attempt on your life despite Katherine's protest, but there hasn't been anything since then. I thought maybe she had succeeded and the danger was past."

"So you kept it from me? You purposely didn't tell me? Hannah, how could you do that?" Seth was practically yelling at me, and Seth never yelled. His arms were flailing in wide gestures as he alternately paced the floor and sent fiery glares my direction.

I remained seated on the floor, almost numbly participating in the argument. This wasn't the first time Seth and I'd had a disagreement. But this was by far the worst.

He'd never been angry at me like this before, but his

rage strangely gave me a bit of a thrill. Seth had agreed to not attempt to shield me from his emotion, and I knew he tried. But I could feel his fear. It was the fear that he would one day do something that would cause me to forever disappear before his eyes. So I often felt that he was still holding back, keeping me at arm's length from himself in order to protect me. This was the first time I knew for sure that I wasn't getting the watered down version of Seth. He was so furious with me that nothing was passing through his normal filter.

"Seth, do you really have room to talk? You're angry with me for not being completely honest, but you have done the same thing to me! And you've done it repeatedly! Do you want me to list all of the times, that I know of, where you have purposely and deliberately withheld the truth from me? All because you were trying to 'protect' me.

"But now I find that you can't be honest, even about something like this? Part of the reason I didn't tell you was because you hadn't told me anything about the project. I didn't know if you had stopped working on it. I was afraid I'd only make things worse by telling you. Even now, you still haven't told me the full story. This could get you killed! Don't I get a say-so? Don't I deserve to know? I'm your wife, Seth!"

"A wife who seems exceptionally good at keeping her own secrets. Don't you think you should have brought this up sooner, say right after you got back from time traveling? You've kept this secret for six months!"

"Are you meaning to tell me that you didn't know? You had no idea this project was dangerous? Did you really think the mugging was random? I'm sorry, Seth, but

I find that very hard to believe."

Seth seemed to deflate. He sat down on the couch as if his strength left with his anger. He rubbed his hands over his face in an anguished motion. "No, I didn't know. I mean, I knew it was potentially dangerous, but I've worked controversial projects before. I suspected it wasn't a random mugging, but I had no evidence that this was the reason. Wayne and Katherine were the only ones who knew about the research and my suspicions."

Seth suddenly stood and began walking toward the kitchen.

"Seth, what are you doing?"

"I'm going to call Katherine."

"No, Seth, you can't!"

"Why not? You said she was trying to protect me."

"But she's on their side! Yes, she was trying to convince them to let her handle the situation, but they're still her clients, and if necessary, she'll protect them, even if that means eliminating the problem—you!"

"I can't believe Katherine would do that. After the mugging, she came to see me and make sure I was okay. She was very upset. Now I realize she was probably even more upset because she knew her clients were behind it. I have to talk to her. Besides, they probably aren't officially her clients any more. She's a state senator now, remember? She won her election a little over a year ago, which would have been about five months after that meeting in Hawaii. She might not be involved with the pharmaceutical company anymore and might be more able to talk about it. She's not going to do anything to put me in danger, and she's the only one who might know how things stand today."

"Seth, she's obviously the one who told them about your research to begin with! Think about it! You said she and Wayne were the only ones who knew. She told them! You can't trust her. That pharmaceutical company probably put her in office! Don't you think they funded her campaign? Besides, even if you do talk to her, what are you going to tell her? You can't say that I overheard their meeting in Hawaii while I was time traveling! Nothing has happened in almost a year and a half. Maybe after the mugging, Katherine got better control of the situation and you're safe now. You said you haven't worked on the project in over a year. Maybe the danger is past. If you bring it up, it might make things worse again. Just let it go, Seth."

"I can't, Hannah." Seth's attitude had transformed from angry to confused and miserable. "I told you I haven't worked on the project. And that was true... up until about a week ago."

"What do you mean?" I asked warily. "You've started working on it again?"

"Just let me explain," Seth said, trying to cut off the objection already on my lips. "I first started researching anti-depressants to find something to help you. Antidepressants work to regulate chemicals in the brain, and I was hoping something similar might keep your tempamine from spiking and triggering time travel. But my analysis of chemical composition of one of the most commonly prescribed antidepressants led me to believe it could cause increasing physical dependence and potentially fatal side effects. I had no test studies, but the problems with the formula seemed obvious. I couldn't imagine the medication being approved even for testing. So I talked to Katherine. Since she specializes in medical law, I thought she might know if there had been any issues brought up with this particular antidepressant. She also might be able to advise me on how to legally proceed with what could be a volatile investigation. I had no idea that Katherine's clients were the pharmaceutical company that produced the medication!

"When I told her about my questions and concerns, she said she'd look into it. A few weeks later, boxes of documented research arrived at the office. Massive numbers of case studies and other research proved that the medication was safe. I thought Katherine had gone a bit overboard, but I appreciated that she'd tried to help me out. After that, I didn't move forward with the project. By that time, we had the formula your mother had created, and I had none of the same concerns about that one. The chemical structure is completely different and would not cause the side effects and dependence I suspected in the other one. So I moved on, figuring I must have been wrong in my initial analysis of the anti-depressant, or that it was just one of those rare instances where something doesn't look good on paper but performs without issue in the real world."

"So I shouldn't have told you!" I interrupted, the regret making me feel sick. "You had moved on by yourself, but now that you know you were right in your concerns, you're not going to let it go."

Seth was silent.

"Please, Seth, don't do this! They'll kill you!"

"Hannah, it's too late. I had already begun working on the project again about a week ago. Wayne and I have increased your dosage of Hannahpren, which seems to be working, but we've also been looking at other options to adjust your medication to be more suitable for your long-term use. Before I had received Katherine's boxes and stopped work on the project before, I had started a few case studies that involved simply observing people who were already taking the antidepressant. I never followed up with them; I didn't really see the point. But when I ran across my project last week, I checked back in with those people involved in the case studies. Hannah, two of my subjects are dead. While their deaths were ruled as natural causes, from talking with their loved ones, I'm fairly certain they both were related to the medication. I can't let this go, Hannah. You've confirmed that this company knows about the problem and is trying to cover it up! That's inexcusable, and they have to be stopped before more people lose their lives!"

"But it's not your fight, Seth! If you get involved, they'll just kill you! They've already tried once!"

"It *is* my fight, Hannah! I'm a doctor. I took an oath that I would do no harm. I can't knowingly allow others to do harm either. If I know about the problem and do nothing, the blood won't just be on their hands, it will be on mine as well. I will not be an accomplice."

"Please, Seth!" My eyes filled with tears, and I could feel my throat constricting. "I heard what they said. You won't get a chance to stop them. They'll kill you. Please, Seth, promise me you won't do it." I knew I was begging. I hated the tone of my voice, and I hated myself for even asking. But I could feel desperation overwhelming me, and I was powerless to stop it. "Seth, if you love me…"

"Hannah, don't ask me. You don't want me to promise

that. I can't. If I let this go, if I let them win, I wouldn't be the man you fell in love with. I can't let them kill people. I have to stand up for what is right, no matter what the cost. It's what God would have me do, and if you think about it, you would never ask me to compromise my integrity by allowing their evil to continue."

He was right. I knew that, but I couldn't make my feelings match what I knew in my head. I focused on breathing in and out, trying to maintain my composure. There had to be some other way—some way to maintain his integrity and do what was right without what seemed to be a suicide mission.

"By now they've already covered up all the evidence," I said, keeping my tone as steady and reasonable as possible. "It will take you years to gather research and case studies to support your theories. As soon as they even suspect you've started working on it again, they'll send someone after you, and this time, I won't know when it will be. You'll die." My face crumpled in a sob. "And I can't... handle... that." I couldn't breathe. Convulsions shook my shoulders as my fragile control was rapidly slipping away.

As I helplessly looked up at Seth through my tears, I saw his eyes widen with fear, as if he suddenly remembered the risk fighting and upsetting me posed. He came forward swiftly and swept me into his arms. "Shhh, Hannah. It's going to be okay. I'm not going to go anywhere. God has taken care of us this far. He hasn't gotten us to this point only to let us go. He was the one who arranged all the bizarre events in your life, remember? He's the one who let you know to save me right in the nick of time. Shouldn't we trust Him with this too?"

"But what are we going to do?" I asked. Though Seth's words were comforting and I had faith that God would continue being God, I needed something immediate to comfort me. I needed to prepare my expectations.

"I'm going to keep working on the project. But I'm going to be smart about it. You're right about Katherine. I won't let her know what I'm doing, but I'll get Wayne's help. Though Wayne knew about this project, it was my research. I hate to potentially put his life at risk as well, but I need him. We'll get some other people on board as well. We'll involve people we can trust and get some immediate advice from a few honorable lawyers as well. I'm sure our silent partner in the Tomorrow Foundation will help us with some of his connections. The more people know about this, even in the research stage, the better. That way, we'll be more difficult to silence. If something happens to one of us, the others will know what to do. My mistake before was in trying to keep quiet until I had evidence. I won't make that mistake again."

The confidence in Seth's voice comforted me more than the words. He wasn't afraid. He knew what to do. He'd been startled by what I'd revealed, but now he was back in control. Seth was smart and capable of handling this. And God was more than capable of handling Seth.

I rested in Seth's arms, letting him support my weight. I suddenly felt drained and weak in the wake of the volatile emotions from the past few minutes.

"I'm sorry, Seth," I whispered against his chest. "I should have told you what had happened right after I came back. If I had, you'd already be that much closer to stopping that company. I was trying to protect you, but I might have just made the situation worse."

"I'm sorry, too, Hannah. You're right. I have a bad tendency of telling you only half-truths. But, trying to protect you like that isn't healthy for either one of us. We need to be able to completely trust each other and know that we are always getting the full story. I'll try to do better, Hannah. I will keep you updated on every detail of the project. But you may have to be patient with me. My first instinct is to always protect you from me, from yourself, or from anything that might do you harm. I love you so much, Hannah."

"Seth, I'm afraid I love you too much! Where you're concerned, I can't think clearly. I'm so sorry!"

"No more sorrys," Seth murmured right before claiming my lips in a kiss that was more effective than any words in letting me know that all was forgiven.

I still felt worry lurking in the back of my head. How would I ever be able to relax knowing that Seth was deliberately putting himself in danger by working on that project?

Fortunately, Seth seemed to be very accomplished at chasing away the shadows, at least temporarily. My knees soon felt weak for another reason, and my husband lifted me up in his arms as he continued to kiss me with increasing passion, erasing all the ugly emotion. With heart pounding, I eagerly returned his kisses, longing to feel the assurance and excitement of his love. The worry, the danger, could wait, but for now, I was learning that the best part of fighting with your husband was getting to make up.

CHAPTER TEN

THERE'S nothing quite like the feeling of finishing your last final exam. And when that final was hopefully the last one you would ever take, that delicious sense of relief is magnified about ten times.

I hummed as I bustled around the kitchen making dinner. I glanced at my cell phone lying on the counter. Seth hadn't called to say he was running late, so that must mean he was still on schedule. I knew I had missed a call from Abby earlier, but she hadn't left a message. I would call her back after dinner. Seth was supposed to be home soon, and I wanted to have the spaghetti ready when he arrived. I also had sparkling apple cider chilling in the fridge and apple pie in the oven as a special treat. I was feeling very accomplished and proud of myself, and I wanted to do something special to celebrate.

After all, I had just finished my Master's degree in Chemistry. Well, I guess I hadn't finished it yet. But all I had left to do was my thesis and the work associated with it. For some students, that would probably be very stressful. But not for me.

I had already completed the rest of the Master's program in record time. Nobody had thought I would be able to finish everything so quickly. I was only a year and a half in and scheduled to graduate in May. Since it was normally a two and a half year program, I had accomplished a lot.

Everyone said I was gifted in the field, but that didn't mean I hadn't worked like crazy. I had spent every waking moment working on this degree, even summers. The only time I'd taken off was for my honeymoon. Thankfully, the university had been wonderful about giving me opportunities to finish the work early. My thesis and the research to go along with it was what I considered the fun part, and I knew it wouldn't be difficult for me.

I didn't particularly enjoy Chemistry, but both Wayne and Seth had assured me that I would enjoy the actual field work I would do with the Tomorrow Foundation. Right now, I was just extremely happy to have my formal classes done and the end in sight.

I think my advisors at the university held out hope that I would continue for my doctorate and maybe even teach. But come May, I was done. After that, my to-do list included working with Seth and Wayne at the Tomorrow Foundation and getting back to my art. This degree had been a necessary chore, and I hadn't had the time to devote to what I felt was my true passion. I even had an open invitation at an art gallery; I just hadn't had the time to create something worthy. My fingers itched to once again hold pencils and paintbrushes, communicating something visible only to my imagination. I had to keep telling myself that it would just be a few more months.

I stirred the spaghetti. Using a spoon from the

silverware drawer, I tasted the sauce. I sighed. It needed a little salt. I wasn't sure why I was even bothering to make spaghetti. Seth was better at it than I was. While I typically did the cooking, Seth was always willing to fill in when he had the time. And he usually did a much better job than I did.

As I put the noodles in the boiling water, I heard the front door open.

"Perfect timing, Seth!" I called. "Dinner should be ready in about eight minutes."

I turned around with a welcoming smile to find Seth standing in the entryway. But he wasn't alone. My dad stood next to him.

"Hi, Dad!" I said, eagerly moving toward them. "This is a nice surprise! I didn't even know you were in the city. Is Mom here too? Let me put some more noodles on. I'm sure we'll have enough for you to join us for dinner."

A third figure moved from behind Seth and Dad. But it wasn't Mom. It was Wayne.

"Wayne, you're here too? Why didn't you guys call and tell…"

The sober expressions on all three faces suddenly registered. Why weren't they smiling? Then I focused on the long needle Wayne held in his hand.

Something was wrong.

"Wayne, what are you doing with that?" I asked cautiously.

Nobody answered.

My heart started pounding, bringing with it an awful,

terrifying sense of foreboding.

"Hannah, you need to stay calm," Seth said as he moved toward me. Wayne was right behind him.

I backed up. "What are you talking about? I am calm!" I felt the refrigerator at my back, blocking further retreat. "Wayne, don't come near me with that thing!"

My gaze swung to Seth. I saw fear. To Wayne. I saw sympathy. To Dad… bone-chilling grief.

Dear, God… no!

Seth spoke, "Hannah, we need to tell you something, but we need to give you something to relax you beforehand." He reached out as if to take me in his arms.

"No!" I said, refusing his comfort. My body was shaking in uncontrollable, shivering spasms. "Somebody just tell me what's going on!"

I focused on my dad, my eyes pleading. His own eyes filled with tears. His voice was hoarse as he finally answered. "Hannah-girl, Abby was driving down from Silver Springs. She must have hit some ice and missed a turn. Her car went off the road."

Dad paused, obviously fighting for control.

"Sweetheart, she didn't make it."

I heard screaming—gut-wrenching, bone-chilling screams. Then I realized they were my own.

Day 1	Day 2	Day 3
The sun rose.	The sun set.	I existed. She didn't.

I'D waited for the blackness. I'd welcomed the nothingness. But it had never come. There was no relief. The world had gone irreparably wrong and would never be right again.

For the past three days I'd been numb—unable to think, unable to feel, and yet I'd felt every single tick of the clock.

"You can't keep her sedated forever, Seth." It was Wayne's voice.

He and Seth were standing at the doorway to our bedroom, discussing me as if I wasn't there, but I kind of wasn't. At least, I hadn't been until now. This was the first time I'd been able to focus outside the numbness to pay attention to those around me.

"If we don't sedate her, she'll time travel. You know she will, Wayne. She can't handle this kind of grief."

"She'll never be able to handle it if you don't let her feel, Seth. Grief has to be worked through. I agreed that we needed to give her something to help with the initial shock. But it's been three days. Hannah is strong. You need to give her a chance."

"This is different, Wayne. Hannah would have an easier time losing a limb as opposed to losing her sister. But you're right. Keeping her sedated is not a permanent solution. I'll have to give her something to get through the funeral, but I won't give her anything after that."

"I think giving her something mild for the funeral is a

good idea," Wayne replied. "She needs to be able to function, but we also don't want her falling apart and disappearing in front of everyone."

The funeral.

I sat up in bed in a sudden panic. "When is it?" I asked. Not waiting for their response, I swung my legs over the bed and stood. I shot a glance at the two men. They were looking at me with shock, mouths hanging open. "When is the funeral?" I repeated.

Blackness began creeping around the edges of my vision, and I felt myself sway. Seth and Wayne sprang into action, each of them rushing to my side and pushing me back down on the bed.

"I must have gotten up too fast," I murmured.

As my vision cleared, I looked back up at them expectantly. "The funeral?" I asked a third time.

In their defense, I don't think I'd uttered a coherent phrase in almost three days. And I somehow doubted the medication was to blame. But the mention of the funeral had pierced through my haze. Reality was marching forward, whether or not I was participating in it. I suddenly remembered my parents, Tom, and all the others who were hurting. I couldn't leave them to shoulder all the responsibility of making arrangements.

"The funeral will be in Sonora at 2:00 this afternoon," Seth finally answered.

I frantically looked at the alarm clock beside the bed. "But it's 8:00! We're going to have to leave right away so I can get there to help with the preparations. Where's Mom? There's so much to do. We need music, right? Don't they usually do some kind of little paper program to hand out at funerals?"

I tried to stand up once again, but Seth put his hands on my shoulders and firmly held me down.

"Slow down, Hannah. You don't have to do a single thing. Everything has been taken care of. Music, photos, program, service, and family potluck afterward—every decision has already been made."

"My poor mom!" I moaned, starting to tear up again. "I should have helped her! I should have…"

"Hannah, it's okay. Your mom had help. She isn't in much better shape than you are. So the rest of us made all the arrangements. Since your mom was unable, your grandma stepped in and took charge. And of course, Tom has had the final say in everything."

"Grandma shouldn't have had to do that. And Tom is probably in no condition to…"

"Everyone has just been concerned about you, Hannah," Wayne spoke up.

I couldn't stand the thought that I was worrying my parents. They had enough sorrow to deal with. They didn't need to be concerned that their other daughter would disappear and die as well.

An overwhelming longing to see my mom suddenly washed over me. But added to that was also the intense desire to take care of her as well.

"I need to see my mom," I said.

"You saw her yesterday," Seth said. "Don't you remember?"

"No."

"Hannah was pretty heavily sedated at the time, Seth," Wayne said. She probably doesn't remember much of anything for the last few days. I've lessened her dosage today, which is probably why she's actually coherent."

Seth shot Wayne an annoyed look. Wayne obviously hadn't okayed any dosing changes through Seth. But I was grateful.

"You'll see her and everyone else at the funeral," Seth assured. "What you need to do now is eat something and get ready. You haven't eaten much in the past three days."

"I'll whip you up something special, Hannah," Wayne announced. "You never say no to one of my creations."

"I'll get the shower started for you," Seth said, turning toward the bathroom.

"Seth?" I called, stopping him.

He turned around.

Seth looked the same. My bedroom looked the same. The world had not changed. But Abby was no longer in it.

"Seth, is she really gone?"

Seth came back to the bed, sat down, and pulled me into his arms. He gently smoothed my hair and decorated it with soft kisses while I buried my face in his strong shoulder.

"I'm so very sorry, Sweetheart. I wish I could say it was all a bad dream, but I can't. Your sister is gone."

CHAPTER ELEVEN

A few hours later, I was watching the passing scenery out the car window as we drove to Abby's funeral. As we headed into the mountains, lazy snowflakes began dancing through the air. It wasn't a heavy snowfall, but enough to brighten the old, packed snow at the sides of the road. Although the area hadn't had a lot of snowfall this year, the tiny flakes served as a gentle reminder that it was winter in the Sierras.

At Seth's insistence, I had already taken an oral medication that was supposed to be relaxing, but I had refused anything stronger. I needed to be able to think and feel something other than the numbness.

I knew this was going to be difficult. I still felt the shock every time my mind recognized that Abby was dead. I still wanted to deny that it was true. Part of me fully expected to turn the corner and see her walking down the street.

But missing the funeral wasn't an option. I needed to be there for both my family and myself. If I didn't attend, I was afraid it would never be real for me.

It was just Seth and me in the car. Wayne had chosen to drive himself. It was a long drive from San Francisco to Sonora, but I had a feeling I was going to need every minute of it to prepare myself. Taking a couple deep breaths, I tried to bravely launch into what I needed to know.

"Seth, what... when... how did it happen?" This was the first time I'd even asked. I'd had such a difficult time comprehending the end result; I hadn't wanted to know any of the details. Knowing would mean acknowledging that it had actually happened. But now, I suddenly had the desire to know everything. I needed to know all the how and whys, both to brace myself for the funeral and to cope with the senselessness of it all.

Without taking his eyes off the road, Seth replied. "Apparently Abby and Tom had some kind of argument. Abby took off in her car. It looks as if she was going too fast around some of the curves, hit some ice, and slid off the road. Her car went down a steep embankment, rolled, and hit a tree. After she left, Tom tried to call her cell phone. He could tell her phone was on because it would ring instead of going straight to voicemail. After trying to reach her about ten times, he decided to go find her himself. When he found the accident, it was already too late. They think Abby was killed instantly."

"And Tom...?"

"Tom's pretty messed up right now. Not only is he grieving for Abby, he's blaming himself. He thinks if they hadn't argued, Abby wouldn't have taken off and would still be alive. I think he's also afraid you and your parents will blame him. He told me things had been tough in their marriage, but he still loved Abby and can't imagine how he's going to live without her."

It would almost be a relief to summon up a righteous anger at Tom. At least then I would have someone to blame. But I couldn't feel angry with him. I had my own guilt to deal with.

If Tom hadn't argued with Abby, maybe she wouldn't have driven off too fast and died. But if I had answered my phone that morning, or even just called her back, maybe she wouldn't have gotten upset at Tom. I had missed that one last conversation with my sister, and now I could never get it back. She had needed me, and I had failed her.

"Abby tried to call me that morning, but I didn't answer," I admitted softly. "She didn't leave a message, but I saw it. I never returned her call."

"Hannah, it's not your fault. There's nothing you could have done. It was an accident."

"But maybe if I had talked to her, I could have calmed her down and she wouldn't have been driving so fast!"

"Abby hasn't been real chatty with you about her personal life lately. Chances are, she was calling you about something unrelated. If it was important, she would have left a message. It probably was before she and Tom even argued. Abby was never one to talk on her cell phone while driving."

"She was also never one to drive too fast! Especially on the Silver Springs road. She was always so careful. I can't imagine her going too fast, even if she was upset. It's not like her."

"We don't know for sure that she was going too fast. She could have hit the ice just right and lost control before she even knew what happened."

"But why were the roads icy? I have weather updates on my phone for that area. I think the last storm they had was about two weeks ago."

"You know the ice never fully melts off that road in the winter. A storm wouldn't be needed for spots to be dangerous, especially the corners."

I was silent, my mind tumbling around all the possibilities and 'what ifs.' And I always went back to the one thought I couldn't shake: If I had answered my phone, Abby wouldn't have died.

"Hannah, you're going to have to let it go," Seth said after several minutes of my brooding. "You're not going to understand it. You'll drive yourself crazy if you try. There is no rhyme or reason. There is nothing you could have done. The only assurance we have is that it didn't catch God by surprise. He's the one you're going to have to trust and depend on to get you through this."

I knew what Seth said was true. But there is a big difference between knowing something in your head and feeling it. Yes, God was in control. So why did he allow such a horrible thing to happen? My sister was dead. I needed someone or something to blame. If I couldn't blame the weather, Tom, myself, or some other third party, the only option left was God.

I didn't say anything to Seth. What would he think if he knew I was developing an anger toward God? Seth was so strong and sure in his faith. Would he be shocked, maybe even repulsed, that I was blaming God? I felt almost ashamed but powerless to stop it. I knew God was real. I knew He was in control of absolutely everything. He was infinite, powerful, all-knowing. He supposedly loved me. I knew he could have easily protected my sister. He could have saved her. So how could I not be angry? He let her die.

What was normally a long drive up into the Sierras passed much too quickly. Before I was ready, we were pulling into the parking lot of the funeral home. Though in all honesty, I don't know that I would have ever felt prepared for my sister's funeral.

The service passed in somewhat of a blur. Seth had insisted I take another pill, and with it, some of the numbness had returned. I felt a sense of detachment, as if I was watching everything from behind a glass window. The funeral was well-attended. Lots of beautiful flowers stood sentinel around the closed casket at the front of the room. A huge spray of red roses graced the top of the modestly ornate wooden casket. Grandma, Seth, and the rest of the family had done a good job with the preparations. Many wonderful things were said about Abby, her favorite songs were played, and there was even a slideshow of photos.

With the help of my sense of numbness, I managed to maintain my composure through everything, but when they started the slideshow, I couldn't watch. Feeling my numb control slipping, I turned away and focused on my hands clasped in my black-skirted lap. I couldn't watch her life replayed without the realization that I would never again see that smile. I couldn't see the photos of Abby and me together without the knowledge that we would never again get to do those things.

At the end of the service, Seth took my elbow as we followed Abby's rose-bedecked casket out of the building. We then joined the long line of cars following the light blue hearse to the cemetery.

I didn't want to talk. If I did, that would mean I'd have to think. And if I thought, that would mean I'd have to process and feel what had just happened. Thankfully, Seth seemed to sense my mood and remained silent. If I could just make it through the graveside service, I could go bury my head under a soft, fluffy pillow and pretend, at least for a while, that none of this had ever happened.

Arriving at the snow-covered cemetery, Seth and I gathered with the rest of my family and friends around a hole that had already been dug and the casket holding my sister's body. A few chairs for the family were positioned on a green mat a few feet from the casket. The rest of the mourners stood. Seth led me to a chair beside my mom and then stood behind me.

It was a peaceful setting. The cemetery was outside of town and nestled up against pine-covered hills. The weak winter sun spread its meager offering over the mourners and the mourned. The gravestones and black-coated people stood in stark contrast against the backdrop of white-covered ground. A snow-muffled hush permeated the scene, seeming both appropriate and a bit unnerving. In such a setting, it almost seemed as if one needed to not speak above a whisper.

The formal service passed quickly with the minister trying to offer comfort in the knowledge that Abby was now with her Savior. He then said a prayer and ended with the traditional, 'Ashes to ashes. Dust to dust.'

The mourners then came forward, pausing in respect at the casket to say their farewells. I remained seated on my hard, cold folding chair, watching as if from a great distance.

The immediate family was the last to go forward. I saw my mom bend down, gently touch the casket, and whisper something no one else could hear. With tears trailing down her face and sobs shaking her body, Dad gently led her away, his own face a mask of grief.

Tom stood for a long moment. I could feel his loneliness, his uncertainty of even how to say goodbye. Finally, he gently kissed his own wedding ring and touched it to the casket. Then he turned and walked away.

Still I sat.

I couldn't seem to make my body move to follow everyone else in paying respects. Seth and I were the only ones still seated. And still I didn't move.

Seth moved in front of me and knelt down to look in my eyes. "Hannah, I don't want to rush you, but the family has arranged for a dinner at the church. I think most everyone else is already headed over there."

I nodded. But I never moved. I just sat staring past him to Abby's box.

I could feel Seth's growing impatience as I clearly ignored him. "Hannah, I need to go help your dad. He wanted to talk to Tom about Silver Springs before he left, since we weren't sure Tom would come to the dinner. Dad wasn't sure how coherent he would be after the service, so he asked if I could help. But I don't feel right about leaving you here."

"I'll stay with her, Seth." It was my grandma's voice. "You go help Dan. Hannah and I will just sit a while."

After a few concerned glances my direction, Seth

complied. Grandma took the seat beside me, picked up my cold hand in her warm one, and started gently stroking it.

When tragedy strikes, people feel the need to offer some sort of comfort, and it seems to usually be in the form of unhelpful platitudes. I had already heard my fair share as people had greeted me before and after the funeral. Phrases like, 'At least you know where she is,' and 'Just picture how happy Abby is right now with Jesus,' I found profoundly uncomforting.

And then there was my favorite: 'You wouldn't want her to have to leave Heaven, even if she could.'

Actually, yes. Yes, I would. I fully admit to being very selfish. And if I could have ripped her away from the throne of glory and brought her back down with me, I would have done it without a second's hesitation.

Thankfully, Grandma seemed to sense some of my feelings. She didn't offer any words of comfort; she just held my hand, letting me know she was right there beside me. Grandma had already been through the grief of losing Grandpa a couple years ago, and perhaps it was this experience that had given her insight into exactly what I needed at that moment.

I might have sat there forever if two of the workers from the funeral home hadn't shown up. As if not seeing us at all, they removed the roses from the casket and started making preparations to lower it into the hole.

Seeing their intention, I suddenly stood to my feet, a cry of protest on my lips.

Gently pulling my hand, Grandma drew me forward and addressed the men.

"I know you're probably in a hurry, but could you give

her just a few more minutes?"

"Oh, sure," the men said, looking as if they'd never even realized our presence. "We'll just wait in the hearse. Take all the time you need."

They left, and I stood with the casket in front of me and the gaping hole beneath it, waiting to claim its newest resident. Grandma stood close with her arm around my back.

I guess I was supposed to say goodbye. But I didn't know how.

It was difficult for me to grasp the fact that Abby's body was actually in there. That blond, bouncy hair, that girl-next door smile, those blue eyes that perpetually sparkled with mischief—were they really silenced forever in that box?

Abby. My Abby. We would never again be able to talk for hours over nothing in particular. Never stay up late eating massive amounts of chocolate and watching sappy romantic comedies. She would never again nose her way into my business and offer her unsolicited advice on any topic. What I would give to have my beautiful, nosy sister back!

Abby and I'd had a bond like no other relationship in my life. If she was really gone, it seems like the sun should stop shining. How could my world continue without her? How could time move forward and the rest of humanity continue as if nothing had changed?

I reached my hand out and touched the cold, heavily-varnished wood. As my fingertips gently caressed the casket, reality surged through me in one overwhelming wave.

I suddenly couldn't breathe. Sobs constricted my throat, choking me even before the tears started. Pure agony ripped through my chest as my mind screamed, "No!"

I slid my arms over the top of the casket, letting it support me. I pressed my cheek against the wood as my tears spread across the surface.

She was gone.

I had delivered her as a baby, been the first person to ever hold her little body. That same baby grew and became my big sister. She'd held my hand as we chased butterflies, blazed the trail of childhood and adolescence, fought my battles, and been my forever best friend. Now that same little body, that same warm little hand, was lifeless and cold in this box.

For the first time in my life, my big sister had gone somewhere I couldn't follow.

They were going to put her in the ground. They were going to take her away from me.

"Don't leave me, Abby! Please. Don't leave." Over and over I moaned pleas to both God and my dead sister.

I was vaguely aware of my grandma standing beside me, gently rubbing my back.

I didn't know if I could survive the pain. As the last of my strength abandoned me, I slid down to my knees on that green mat surrounding the burial area, and I rested my forehead against the side of the box.

The fierceness of my sobs lessened, leaving me shuddering for breath and practically writhing with what seemed to be a physical, searing pain where my heart was supposed to be. I didn't want to leave her alone in that cold, dark grave. If I got up and said goodbye, it would almost seem an acceptance of something that was completely wrong. I'm sure someone with more sense than I would say that Abby wasn't really there, that she didn't need me anymore. And my brain recognized that as true. But I needed her. And the thought of leaving her lifeless body was too much to bear.

At some point, I stopped feeling Grandma's gentle touch on my back, and I was grateful. I knew she wouldn't be far away, but it was somewhat of a comfort to just be alone. My breathing finally slowed as I rested against the casket with my eyes closed.

It was as if I was in the eye of a storm.

Then the tears once again began flowing. But these weren't the great, wracking sobs of protest. They were the soft, sorrowful tears of deep, helpless grief. I bent my head down to the mat, almost in a position of prayer. I wanted to pray, but I couldn't find the words. All I could manage was a simple, "Help," as I rocked back and forth in misery.

At some point my tears stopped and the moisture dried on my face. I don't know that it was acceptance so much that I was empty. I had nothing left. Abby was dead. Yes, there was a small measure of peace that beckoned me with the renewed assurance that Abby really wasn't in that coffin. I wasn't leaving her. God was taking care of her in heaven better than I ever could here on earth. That didn't mean that I wasn't still very confused and angry. I just think that when you've given it all and come to the end of your rope, God grants you enough comfort, faith, and peace to breathe your next breath… and then the next one after that.

I gradually became aware of a cold wetness seeping through my skirt and down the length of my legs. As I blinked and opened my eyes, my vision began to clear and I realized rather dully that I was kneeling in snow.

Confused, I raised my gaze.

There was no green mat... no casket... no hole.

Tombstones stretched out across the cemetery, their gray heads peeking above the blanket of white. But in front of me, the snow was unbroken.

CHAPTER TWELVE

I sat in the same position for a long time, just staring. I was waiting to feel something. Waiting to feel shock, surprise, maybe even fear. Waiting for my heart to start pounding and panic to overtake me. But it didn't.

I knew I had time traveled. But I couldn't seem to summon up the energy to care.

The snow soaked my skirt and tights. The discomfort is what finally roused me enough to try to stand on my now-tingly legs.

Then I started walking. I didn't have a plan or a destination. I didn't look at the scenery, and I couldn't even say what I was thinking. I just walked. I think I made a couple turns in my aimless wandering, but since I was outside of town, there weren't many buildings to serve as location marks. There weren't any sidewalks either. I just walked at the side of the road with my gaze fixed straight in front of me.

The area was rural and beautiful with haphazard trees lining the streets and a terrain that extended into surrounding hills and mountains. But it was as if I was lost in my own mind and wasn't even aware of putting one foot in front of the other. So much had happened that I couldn't seem to process that I had potentially landed myself in serious danger. I just had nothing left.

I finally realized I was trembling. My feet stopped moving, and I looked around in confusion. I had no idea where I was. Shadows were lengthening. The sun retired early in the mountains, making it dangerous to be out in the open at night. Already, the wetness of my clothes made the dropping temperature even more miserable. I looked down at my feet. I couldn't feel my toes. Although the roads had been plowed, I had walked through the snow at the cemetery in my nice black pumps. While they were a warmer, sturdier variety than some heels, they definitely weren't appropriate wear for hiking through snow drifts and long walks on icy roads.

What was I going to do? Although I still couldn't muster up enough energy to care much, I also wasn't ready to just give up and die. My survival instincts seemed to finally kick my brain into motion. Although I still wasn't even close to my usual time travel panic, I did suddenly realize exactly how much danger I was in. If I was going to live past this time traveling jaunt, I needed to find some shelter, I needed to get somewhere Seth or Wayne could find me to administer the medicine when I returned to my correct time, and I needed to do all that without my wallet or any cash.

After my little side-trip on our honeymoon, I had been more than a little paranoid about suddenly time traveling without necessary resources, such as money… and clothes. Fortunately, Seth had been very understanding and more than a little paranoid as well. He insisted I keep my wallet on my person as much as humanly possible.

Unfortunately, I hadn't taken it out of the car at the graveside service. My skirt hadn't afforded an unobtrusive place to carry it on me, and then, with Seth watching me so closely and the relaxing medication in my system, I really hadn't thought I would time travel.

I slowly began walking again. If I was going to survive, I needed to keep moving. But now that I was aware of my surroundings and the cold, it was much more difficult to keep at a steady pace. I had no idea how far out of town I was. There was no traffic. The entire time I'd been walking, I'd only seen one car, and it was turning the opposite direction.

As I walked, I shed the last traces of apathy, and in its place came the fear. I thought I was headed in the right direction toward town, but I had no idea if I would make it before complete darkness had descended. There were a few houses scattered around, but they were all off the road behind a thick wall of trees and bushes. Did I even dare try to knock on a stranger's door to get some help?

Desperation was clawing at my heels. I didn't have the emotional strength to handle yet another crisis. I really wanted to just curl up in a ball at the side of the road, cover my eyes and ears, and try to imagine away my reality.

A fresh sob gagged me as I realized that, while I'd had some difficult moments in my life, this had to be the worst. Yes, I had come very close to dying before, but that was entirely different than losing someone you love. And yes, I'd been stuck out of my own time before, but at least I'd always had resources or friends to work with. But at this specific moment in my life, my sister was dead, I had traveled through time to who knows when, I had no money, I was wet and stranded with freezing night approaching, and I would very likely die either from exposure or from traveling back to my own time.

My feet stopped moving as I once again considered the advantages of just curling into a ball and giving up. I had reached my limit. Shudders raked through my body. Weakness threatened to buckle my knees.

"God!" I moaned, closing my eyes and begging for some relief from the pain and hopelessness. "I can't... *Where* are You?"

It was half angry demand and half plea.

Where had He been when Abby had died? Where was He now when I desperately needed help?

And then, as if the breeze was speaking audibly, a complete verse of scripture whispered through my mind.

'I lift up my eyes to the hills

From where does my help come?

My help comes from the Lord

Who made heaven and earth.'

I was so startled I actually looked up at the hills around me and turned a complete circle. Then my eyes came to rest on a small sign about thirty feet in front of me.

It was small and a bit faded, but the black lettering clearly said, 'Prospector Shuttle Service.'

My heart gave a mighty leap, assuring me that it actually was still functioning. I began walking toward the sign as fast as my numb feet could take me.

How had I missed the sign before? But I already knew the answer. I hadn't been looking up, literally. I'd been walking with my head down, so focused on my problem that I hadn't been looking for the solution.

I breathed a quick prayer of thanks. My life should have taught me before now not to short-change God. Everything I'd been through had proven the minute detail with which God masterfully worked. He who made the heaven and earth was more than capable of handling my problems. But just because I could recognize God's provision didn't mean I wasn't still angry with Him for some of His choices. He'd just helped me, so why couldn't He have helped Abby to make that curve and live?

I arrived at the sign and turned to look up the lane. I could see the outline of a building through the trees, but it certainly didn't look like a professional storefront. I wasn't in a commercial district either. While the thought of venturing up that drive and talking to strangers was a little unnerving, I didn't really have a choice.

I started up the snow-packed lane, but as the building came into full view, I panicked. It was a house, and though I realized it might simply be a home-based business, it did increase my misgivings. The real problem, however, was that I suddenly realized, even if this was a legitimate shuttle service that could take me to San Francisco, I had no way to pay them.

I frantically reached down to search my pockets, though I'm not sure what I expected to find. Lint wasn't going to be able to pay for anything. Surprisingly, my left hand came in contact with something unexpected. I pulled what felt like a rolled up wad of papers from my pocket.

I gasped. It was a large, rolled up wad of cash.

I then actually let out a half-giggle and whispered,

'Thanks, Seth!"

Seth loved surprises. Specifically, he took great pleasure in planning extravagant, sometimes bizarre, surprises for me. I hated surprises, and while I usually didn't appreciate his efforts, my sweet husband had developed one method which I did like. Every once in a while, Seth would slip something into my purse or the pocket of my coat for me to find later. Sometimes it was cash meant for me to spend as I pleased. A few times it was jewelry or some other small gift. Once or twice it was a simple love note he'd written for me. After the first time I'd washed thirty dollars in cash through the washing machine, I'd complained to Seth. He'd simply smiled and said I'd better start the habit of checking pockets before throwing things in the washing machine.

I quickly counted the wad of bills; then, shocked, I recounted them. $200. Seth had put $200 in my pocket. He had never left me that much cash before. Maybe he'd been worried about me time traveling and wanted to make sure I'd have money on my person just in case, or maybe he'd just wanted to give me an extra surprise. No matter how and why the money had gotten in my pocket, it served as an answer to prayer right now.

I didn't know what a 'shuttle service' would actually entail, but it would hopefully get me to San Francisco for less than $200.

I stuck the money back in my pocket, and walked toward the house. It definitely did not look like a business. It was a nice, two-story house, but it was older and hadn't been fully maintained. Paint was peeling off the exterior, and a collection of older cars in various conditions was parked around the front yard, almost making it appear to be an old junkyard. Before I reached the porch, a man, probably hearing the crunch of snow beneath my feet, stuck his head out from the hood of a rusty, old pickup and looked at me. He had a scruffy gray beard and looked to be in his late forties or early fifties. It was below freezing outside, and yet the large man was working in a grease-stained T-shirt, tattered jeans, and a Giants baseball cap. He might have looked frightening except that his expression was friendly.

"Hi, Miss. Can I help you?"

"Yes. The sign on the road said something about a shuttle service? I need a ride to San Francisco."

"Dad!" the man suddenly yelled, his gaze never leaving me. "You have a customer!"

Less than ten seconds later, an older man rounded the corner of the house. He would probably be considered elderly. I would have guessed him to be closing in on eighty years old, but he carried himself like a young man. His gait was strong and sure and his posture erect. Although his hair was wispy white and his clean-shaven face bore the map of age in wrinkles, his icy blue eyes were direct and clear.

"You need a shuttle service, Miss?" he asked as he approached me.

"Yes, I need a ride to San Francisco."

"When do you need to leave?"

"Right now," I answered miserably. I tried to come up with some reasonable explanation as to why I would show up on foot, looking like something the cat had drug in, and requesting immediate transportation from the area, but I couldn't come up with anything. So I remained silent and tried to hold his gaze steady as he seemed to look right through me in his scrutiny.

"Alright then. We'd better get a move on." He turned to his son. "I'll go ahead and take the truck instead of the van, Bobby. I have to be in the city tomorrow anyway to pick up that load for the Snellings. I'll just stay overnight and be back mid-morning tomorrow."

He took some keys out of his pocket and gestured for me to follow him. We walked behind the house to where a newer, fully-equipped red truck was parked. He grabbed some kind of sign leaning against the side of the house and placed it on top of the truck. As he got it in position, I saw that it was one of those plastic, triangular placards like are used on pizza delivery cars. This little sign said 'Prospector Shuttle' and looked rather ridiculous perching atop the big truck.

"I'm Charlie Brown, by the way," he said conversationally as he backed up to survey his work. "I'm the owner of Prospector Shuttle."

"Charlie Brown? Are you serious?" I asked, incredulous.

He smiled. "Yep, just like the cartoon. But I think I still have a bit more hair than the little guy."

I extended my hand to meet his offered one.

"Hi. I'm Hannah."

As our hands briefly shook, Charlie studied me with a thoughtful expression, almost as if he recognized me from somewhere but couldn't quite remember where. However, his thoughtful expression could also have been due to my bedraggled appearance. I probably looked and seemed more than a little strange. After all, I'd shown up on foot in a skirt, blouse, and pumps, and my make-up was probably smeared all over my face and around my puffy, red-rimmed eyes.

He suddenly cocked a grin at me and turned to open the passenger side door with a flourish. "Hope you don't mind us taking the Red Barron instead of the van.

The Red Barron was a great name for the big truck. "Of course I don't mind. I'm just happy to get a ride." I started to step up into the truck and stopped. "Um... Mr. Brown, how much do I need to pay you for this?"

"Call me Charlie. 'Mr. Brown' makes me feel like an old man. Our policy is that you don't pay until we get you where you're going. Then you pay us what you feel the drive was worth."

While that sounded like a refreshingly old-fashioned policy, it made me extremely nervous. I didn't even have a ballpark estimate of what I should pay. What if I didn't have enough money?

"So what is a drive like that usually worth?" I asked cautiously.

"Oh, with the cost of gas and everything, we generally like to get around $190 to go to San Francisco."

I nodded. I'd have just enough money.

I hopped up into the nice leather seats of The Red Barron while Charlie shut my door and went around to the driver's side.

We were soon on the road, and I breathed a sigh of relief. This was going to work. I was going to make it to San Francisco, and then I could relax and go back to my own time, whenever that was. Now I just had to avoid revealing too much to Charlie on the multi-hour drive.

Unfortunately, Charlie wasn't going to make that easy. "You know, usually our customers call and schedule to be picked up. I've been doing this shuttle service for ten years now, and this is the first time I've had a customer show up at our door with wet feet and no luggage."

I still had no explanation. Every lie I could think of sounded absolutely ridiculous. So I said nothing and just pretended an obsessive interest in the scenery out my window.

Fortunately, Charlie pulled into a gas station to fill the tank, and I was able to momentarily escape further scrutiny. As he got out, my glance caught on some small papers sitting in between the seats. It was a neat stack of old gas receipts. I hurriedly picked one up and looked for the date stamp. Finding it, I breathed a sigh of relief. One year. I had only slipped back in time one year.

I searched my brain, trying to remember my life from a year ago. I was going to need some help and a destination when I got to San Francisco. We wouldn't arrive until after dark, and I would have no money left to get a hotel room. My head hurt as I tried to remember where everyone was a year ago.

Seth and I were engaged. I was going to school. Mom and Dad were in negotiations about selling their house. With the date being so close to Christmas, Seth and I weren't even in San Francisco. We had gone to his parents' house near Monterey for Christmas.

Even if I was able to, I couldn't go to Seth for help. With the engagement, Seth and I were constantly with each other. I couldn't risk running into myself, and I also couldn't risk Seth finding out I'd time traveled again. If he knew, he might take measures to prevent me traveling back in time on our honeymoon. That could cause some serious timeline issues. Besides, if I hadn't gone back, I would have never known about the potential threat to Seth's life.

So if I couldn't get help from Seth, what was I going to do once I spent all my money to reach San Francisco?

Charlie opened the driver's side door and climbed back into the truck. After stopping for some fast food, where I spent $6 of my remaining $10 for a burger and fries, we were back on the road. I would have just skipped dinner, but I hadn't eaten anything since breakfast. As it was, I inhaled the meal so fast I didn't really taste it.

"So what brought you to Sonora?" Charlie asked.

Normally, Charlie's friendly, direct manner would have put me at ease. But I didn't want to talk. Unfortunately, I got the impression that he wasn't going to be satisfied with a long, silent drive. He was curious. He wasn't going to give up until I gave him some answers.

"A funeral," I said simply. Maybe if I kept my answers brief, he would get the hint and stop trying to start a conversation.

"My condolences," he replied. But apparently that wasn't enough information to satisfy him. "And you didn't have a ride afterward?"

"I stayed longer than the others. I guess we got our timelines mixed up, so I had to get my own ride."

I tried to come up with something else to say before Charlie asked his next question. I needed to find a way to divert the conversation away from me.

Charlie opened his mouth, but I launched in, cutting him off with the first thing that popped into my head. "So your name is Charlie Brown. You drive a truck you call the Red Barron. Do you also have a beagle named Snoopy?"

"Snoopy the 5th died recently. He was a good dog. I haven't yet had the heart to find Snoopy the 6th.

"You've had five dogs named Snoopy?"

Charlie shrugged. "It's a good name. My wife had a yellow canary for a while that she called Woodstock."

"And I suppose your wife's name is Lucy?"

"No. My wife passed away several years ago. Her name was Rose. But there was this red-haired girl once…" He shot a pointed, ornery glance at my red hair and wiggled his eyebrows.

I laughed. "That's right. Charlie Brown always had a thing for the little red-haired girl."

My laugh sounded foreign to my ears, and for some reason, it reminded me of why I hadn't laughed in a while. And the grief and depression descended over me like a cloud once again.

Charlie, seeming to sense the change in my mood, refrained from asking more questions and instead turned on the radio to an oldies station. As we descended out of the Sierra Mountains, I dully watched out the window, trying to keep my mind from dwelling on my problems and my loss. If I broke down in front of Charlie, there would be no end to the questions.

I was usually quite paranoid of letting other people drive, and having someone I didn't know chauffeur me on a multi-hour trip was enough to send me into a panic attack. But for once, I didn't have my typical reaction. When we first left Sonora, I was still so wrapped up in my own grief, I wasn't really processing things normally.

At some point, though, I discovered plenty of distraction in Charlie Brown.

Every time a new song came on, Charlie would state the title, the artist, and the year the song was released. It was fascinating, hilarious, and charming all at the same time. Charlie would then proceed to sing all of the lyrics, mostly in tune and mostly on high volume.

I'd heard the phrase, 'Dance like no one's watching.' Well, Charlie sang like no one was listening! Or maybe at his age, he was comfortable enough with himself that he simply didn't care who was listening! Either way, watching and listening to his antics provided plenty of entertainment and thoroughly amused me despite my depression.

The first few measures of a song began.

" 'House of the Rising Sun,'" Charlie announced. " 'The Animals.' 1965."

"1964," I corrected.

Charlie threw me a shocked expression. "1964?" He paused, thinking. "You're right! It was 1964! How did you know that?"

I shrugged. "My grandparents always had classic oldies playing in their house when I was growing up. And, of course, if we ever went anywhere in the car with them, we only ever listened to music from before 1980. They had some old records, and then they got more modern with some audio cassettes. They especially liked this collection that had all of the number one hits arranged by year.

'House of the Rising Sun' was on the 1964 cassette."

Charlie laughed. "And do you know all the lyrics, Miss Hannah?"

"Of course," I answered, though I don't know that I'd ever admitted it to anyone or found a use for my vast knowledge. I then rather timidly joined him in singing the lyrics.

For the remainder of the drive, Charlie got ridiculous joy out of quizzing me each time a new song came on. We got in a few mild arguments over the dates. It was blessedly unimportant, and I loved it. By the time we reached San Francisco, I was belting out every lyric in a loud duet with Charlie Brown. And I was singing like no one was listening.

CHAPTER THIRTEEN

THE Red Barron pulled away, leaving me alone on the dark street. When Charlie had asked where in the city to take me, I had given him directions to Wayne's townhouse. Wayne was the only person I could think of who would understand and help me. If I remembered right, Wayne had stayed in the city over Christmas last year and had gone for the day to visit his parents and have dinner at his sister's house.

I had given Charlie all of my $194, assured him that this was the right place, and sent him on his way, but now, as I looked up at the dark building, I had sudden misgivings. I had never actually been inside Wayne's townhouse. I knew where it was and had dropped Seth off here several times, but Wayne usually came to our place.

I slowly walked up the front steps to the door. Thankfully, my clothes had thoroughly dried on the drive, though my tights still felt a bit squishy in my shoes.

I didn't even know for sure that Wayne was home, or that he'd be coming home tonight. He often worked late at the Tomorrow Foundation, but I certainly didn't keep track of the man's habits or schedule.

But Wayne was my only option.

I rang the doorbell. It didn't seem like there were any lights on inside, but I still hoped against hope that the blinds were just drawn across the windows.

I waited. No one opened the door, and I heard no movement either. After several long minutes, I desperately tried the door. It was locked.

Sighing in discouragement, I backed up into the shadows and sat with my back against the corner of the porch. Maybe if I just waited, Wayne would show up. He had to come home eventually, right?

The hard cement offered no cushioning for my rear, and bricks at my back seemed to bite into me like sharp little teeth. Yet I still managed to slip into the twilight stage, hovering between sleep and awake. There wasn't a lot of traffic on this street, and the more distant noise of the city seemed to fade to background noise. Maybe if I just slipped a little more, lost the last bit of awareness, I would relax into my own time.

The sound of a key in the lock startled me alert.

"Wayne," I called weakly.

Wayne jumped straight up about six inches, swiveled around, and landed in a comical defensive stance with his hands blocking his face. Then his arms dropped and he straightened, as if the sound of my voice suddenly registered.

"Hannah?" He rushed over, bending over me in concern. "Hannah, what are you doing here?"

"I seem to be having some time issues," I replied. "I'm

a bit misplaced at the moment."

By his silence, I knew he'd understood exactly what I'd meant.

I was so cold. I tried to say something else, but my teeth were chattering so badly I couldn't. I didn't know how long I'd been sitting there, but San Francisco wasn't exactly tropical. Even with a coat, the moisture from the bay could create a chill that seemed to seep directly into your bones.

"Come on, Hannah. Let's get you inside."

Wayne helped me up, and I was able to make my stiff feet move enough to walk into the house with his assistance.

He turned on the lights as we went, their sudden brightness momentarily blinding me. He led me to the couch, gently pushed me into it and then took off my shoes. Finding a blanket, he wrapped me in it, and then disappeared for several minutes.

"You're still shivering, Hannah, and your feet are wet. You should probably go take a hot shower to get warmed up. I put a T-shirt and some sweatpants in the bathroom for you."

It wasn't until I'd been standing under the hot water for several minutes that I started to lose the fog around my mind and I began to feel warm. I stayed in the cocoon of the shower for a long time, not wanting to leave and deal with the problems and questions outside the curtain.

After giving myself ten last blissful seconds in the hot fountain, I resolutely turned it off and stepped out. I shrugged into Wayne's comfortably large clothes, dried my hair with his dinky little hair drier, and left the bathroom to find Wayne eating a bowl of cereal at the breakfast bar.

Wayne had a nice, comfortable townhouse, though it was a little lacking in the home décor department. It was pretty sparse—a typical bachelor pad. The couch and recliners were comfortable and the TV was huge. Overall though, Wayne's homemaking skills were very pleasantly surprising. For a single adult guy, his home was surprisingly neat and clean.

I slid onto the barstool beside him, trying to figure out exactly what to say and what not to say about my unexpected presence. The silence stretched out to several minutes as Wayne continued to shovel the cereal into his mouth. Finally reaching the last bit, Wayne pushed the empty bowl away and turned to me.

"So… you come here often?"

I busted out laughing. Wayne's sense of humor and ability to make me laugh in the tensest situations was one of my favorite things about him.

"No," I answered. "At least, I certainly try not to."

"Past or future?" he asked.

"Alright, Wayne, I'll say what you want to hear: 'I come from the future.'"

Wayne smiled, his dark blue eyes twinkling. He had always had somewhat of a delighted fascination with my time travel. It was a much too-close reality to his love of science fiction.

"But only a year in the future. So don't get your hopes up."

"No, it's okay. I think one year is enough. Let's see, I

need the winners for the Superbowl, the NBA finals, the World Series, the Stanley Cup,… Oh, and the Kentucky Derby as well"

I smiled. "What's really amusing, Wayne, is that you seem to think I actually know the winners for all those."

"Okay, maybe not. But surely you know who wins the Superbowl?"

I remained silent, simply raising my eyebrows at his antics.

Wayne sighed dramatically. "We really need to work on your education, Hannah." Then, turning serious, his brow creased. "So if you're time traveling again, that means we need to adjust your medication. We knew it was a possibility that you would develop a slight tolerance for the Hannahpren, but if I just adjusted…"

"Wayne, you can't. I came to you because I had no choice. But you have to forget I was even here. If you do anything to adjust my medications or do anything differently because of my presence, then you'll change events that have already happened for me. It'll make a bigger mess than what I'm already dealing with. You have to let events play out as if you don't know that I will time travel again."

Wayne had always had the amazing ability to switch effortlessly between the serious, brilliant Dr. Hawkins and the easy-going, quirky, funny man he was. I knew this was going to be difficult for him. If there was a problem, he was used to fixing it. And he was used to telling Seth everything. Those two didn't have secrets. Asking him to keep a secret and not solve a problem for a year was going to be a monumental task for him.

"You're right." Wayne said. "We need to get you back to your own time as soon as possible. The longer you're here, the more chance you have of disrupting the timeline. Have you done anything to change anything yet? I know you've changed stuff when you've time traveled before, but that was stuff you did rather inadvertently, almost as if God had sent you there for that specific purpose, right? Was there anything like that this time?"

"No, I'm pretty sure this one isn't a mission from God. Something bad happened. I got very upset. Next thing I know, I had slipped back a year." I so wanted to tell him what had happened! But if we were going to try to mess up the future as little as possible, I needed to give him as little information as possible. I wasn't exactly familiar with the ethics of time traveling, but I figured that unless God made it clear that I was supposed to change something, I needed to leave as little imprint on the past as possible.

"Okay, so how can I help get you 'back to the future'?" The teasing Wayne was back.

"You've already helped. I needed to be close to either you or Seth so that, when I do go back, one of you will be around to keep me from dying. So in a year, you'd better have a nice stockpile of Karisenol waiting for me. Other than that, there's no exact science. You know I travel back when I relax, so that will probably happen as I relax to go to sleep. At least, that's when it usually does."

"And you're sure you don't need like a lightning storm or 1.21 gigawatts of electricity to make it happen?"

"No, but I better get out of here soon. I don't know how many more time travel jokes I can take."

"You can go to bed any time you want," Wayne said.

"I can sleep out here on the couch and you can take my bed."

"No, you keep your bed. I'll take the couch. I'm supposed to relax, and that won't happen if I take your bed. Besides, a year from now, it will be much better for me to wake up on your couch than to wake up in bed with you!"

"Ha! I didn't even think of that!"

"I've learned a few things about my time traveling the hard way. Never relax somewhere that would get you in trouble in your original time. And always wear clothes."

"You're going to make me wait a year to hear that story, aren't you?"

After I drank a glass of milk and borrowed a new toothbrush from Wayne's last visit to the dentist, Wayne and I made a bed on the couch for me. I immediately lay down on the fluffy pillow, and Wayne gently tucked me in, pulling the blanket up to my chin.

I watched him, my eyelids already feeling heavy. His eyes were shadowy, and the brown waves of his hair reflected a rich color in the dim light from the lamp placed on the end table. His tall frame bent over the couch, making sure the blankets were in place and each wrinkle was flattened to be the most comfortable possible for me. Next to Seth, Wayne was the smartest, most handsome, sweetest man I knew. What would I have done without him? God had truly blessed me with his friendship.

"Good night, Hannah," Wayne said, smiling gently as he touched off the light on his way to his own room.

"Good night, Wayne," I replied. "Thank you. I'll see you in a year."

I didn't even remember falling asleep. It was if someone turned off a light switch, and I was lost in a numb, dreamless sleep.

I heard a faint sound that gradually pulled me from the depths of sleep like a bucket being drawn up from a deep well. I opened my eyes a slit, the light seeming to increase as I surfaced. I saw the outline of Wayne standing beside the couch with his arms folded.

I sat up.

Wayne looked down at me, "Well, that didn't work."

CHAPTER FOURTEEN

IT was official. I was stuck.

I sat in front of the TV, waiting for Wayne to get home and watching a sappy romantic comedy and feeding my misery with a bowl of popcorn and a bag of chocolate chips.

It had been a month, and I still hadn't traveled back to my right time. I knew I had to be getting on Wayne's nerves. After all, I hadn't left his house by myself in thirty days. I'd been too afraid that I'd run into myself or my family or that I'd do something to screw up the timeline. So I'd stayed inside, eating Wayne's food, watching his TV, sleeping on his couch, and hoping that it would just eventually happen.

It wasn't like we hadn't tried to get me to time travel. A couple times, Wayne had insisted on escorting me on a walk, thinking the fresh air and physical exercise would be good. I'd bundled up, using a scarf and sunglasses as a disguise, but it hadn't done the trick. I'd read a lot of books, eaten massive amounts of chocolate, slept more than I had in my entire life, and even tried the relaxation videos Wayne had procured. In desperation, I'd even consented to take a mild muscle relaxant at Dr. Hawkins' suggestion, but the only thing it succeeded in doing was making me feel so dopey that I vowed never to try it again.

I missed Seth. I knew he would be worried sick about me being gone for a month, and that guilt didn't help me either. The lonely days were tough, but the nights were even worse. I longed to feel Seth lying beside me, to sleep with his arms around me.

I looked at the clock.

Wayne had been working late again. Sometimes I wondered if he did it because he was trying to avoid me. I knew it couldn't be easy on him. He had to keep my secret while trying to appear normal every day for Seth and the other Hannah. The stress was getting to me. I knew that every day added more risk that I was altering the future. What if Wayne was working on some important project, but because of the stress of my presence, made some mistake that he hadn't made originally? The possibility for disasters was endless.

I tried to be as little a burden as possible and to do my part to help Wayne. I did some of the cooking along with all of the cleaning and his laundry, but it somehow didn't seem enough. I was profoundly bored and worried, and yet I knew neither one of those emotions was going to help my odds of time traveling. But the more I tried to stop feeling stressed, the more stressed I became.

I heard Wayne's key in the door. I stood as he came in looking tired and weary. At this point, he was no longer surprised to see me still around when he came home.

"Hi, Wayne, have you eaten? I already ate, but I could

fix you a plate of something?"

"No, I'm fine, Hannah. I already ate at the big banquet meeting we had with the donors.

Wayne took off his coat, and I saw he was wearing a formal suit.

"Oh, was that today? I remember going to that with Seth."

"Yes, you were there, or rather the other Hannah was."

"Do you want to play a game or watch a movie?" I asked hopefully, knowing how pitiful I sounded. But I was so bored and lonely I couldn't help myself. "I already made some popcorn."

"Sure," Wayne replied, though his tone was a little less than enthusiastic. Sometimes I got the distinct impression that Wayne had no idea what to do with me. "I'd be fine with a movie. But not one of your lovey-dovey nonsense. Choose a sci fi or an action. Just let me go change my clothes first."

Relieved, I hurried to find something while he was in his bedroom. Thankfully, Wayne usually consented to play a game or watch something with me before going to bed. Sometimes I felt it was the only thing that kept me sane after being alone all day.

When Wayne returned, we sat on the couch, ate popcorn, and watched some alien doomsday movie I had absolutely no interest in. About three-quarters of the way through, I felt myself dozing, although how I could still be tired, I had no idea. I fought it for a while, but then I finally gave up and let my head droop against something soft beside me.

Wayne jumped off the couch as if he'd been stung by a bee, and I realized too late that I'd been leaning against him.

"I think we might as well turn it off and go to bed, Hannah, especially if you're going to sleep through it."

"Okay," I replied, shocked and immediately pressing the button on the remote to stop the movie. I looked at him, thoroughly confused and trying to figure out what had upset him so much. Wayne had never been cross with me before, and yet over the past few weeks, I'd felt an increasing tension from him.

"Wayne, what's wrong?" I asked. I didn't like the thought of him being upset with me. "Something is obviously bothering you. Are you mad at me for some reason? I know I've probably long over-stayed my welcome."

Wayne sighed, shut his eyes briefly, and then returned to perch on the other side of the couch from where I was sitting.

"I'm not mad at you, Hannah. I know it's not your fault. I won't lie though. It is very stressful having you here. I feel like I have to lie every day I go to work. It's weird, to say the least, seeing the other Hannah at work and knowing you're here. I've had to stop myself countless times from referring to something she wouldn't know about. I just wish we could find a way to get you back to the right time."

"I know. I'm sorry," I said, feeling tears stinging my eyes. "We've already tried everything I can think of."

"This hasn't ever happened before? You've never been stuck?"

"No. I've never been gone from my own time for longer than a few hours. Never more than over-night, and certainly nothing like this. I'm not sure what to do."

Wayne was silent, and then, hesitantly, he said, "Whatever happened to send you back in the first place must have been pretty traumatic. So traumatic, maybe subconsciously, you don't want to go back."

I stared at him, feeling tears pool in my eyes and make long trails down my cheeks. He was right. I had spent the last month avoiding thinking about what awaited me in my own time. I thought if I ignored it, I'd be able to relax and time travel. If I thought about it, I would have to process what had happened. I didn't know that I would ever be able to come to terms with it. The mere thought of having to deal with the trauma made me afraid I'd never be able to return."

"Maybe if I told you what happened, maybe that would help me deal with it," I said softly. Then I brightened. "Or if I tell you, maybe you could actually prevent it from happening! Then I wouldn't have a problem going back. Everything would be as it should be!"

Wayne adamantly shook his head. "You can't do that, Hannah. You can't tell me what happened, and you can't expect me to change your history. It's too dangerous. I might mess things up even worse."

"But it's someone's life!"

"And if I try to fix it, maybe more lives will be lost!" Wayne had probably already figured out by now that someone had died, and yet, he wasn't willing to do anything to prevent it.

Seeing my expression, Wayne lowered his voice and

tried to explain. "Every time you've changed something, you yourself have done it directly, and you've been in the right place at the right time to do it. If God had wanted you to change this, he would have sent you back to the time when you yourself could have made the changes and maybe even given you the assurance that this was what you were supposed to do. You can't expect me to take over God's job, Hannah. He's the one in charge of history. Not me. Not you. I won't mess with it."

I was silent.

"You're going to have to find a way to deal with this, Hannah. Maybe we need to find you a counselor or something. I don't know. I've been there for the nightmares. Remember? You're not dealing with this, and I think the only way you're going to make it back to your own time is if you do."

My mind flashed back to the nights over the past month when I'd woken Wayne with my crying and screaming. Every time, he'd come and held me on the couch until I'd woken enough to get control. He'd never asked me about the nightmares, and this was the first time he'd even mentioned them. But I'd remembered them. I shuddered just thinking about the grotesque ways in which I'd watched Abby die in my dreams.

"This isn't your today, Hannah. You don't belong here, and you're going to create an even bigger catastrophe if you don't get yourself back where you belong."

"What if I don't like my today," I whispered, studying my hands.

"I think that's something you're going to have to take up with God," Wayne replied gently. Then he stood, and, after placing a soft kiss on my forehead, he whispered, "Goodnight," and left for his own room.

I sat there for a long time with tears streaming down my face. I knew Wayne had been right about everything. As uncomfortable and depressing as it was to be stuck here, there was one thing about this time that I couldn't seem to give up. Abby was alive.

I glanced over at the phone. Then I looked at the clock. I knew she would still be up.

Before I had a chance to second guess myself, I picked the phone up and dialed the number. This wasn't the first time I'd used the phone. This wasn't the first time I'd called her. But I'd never admit it to Wayne. He was too worried about me messing up the timeline. He wouldn't approve, and he definitely wouldn't understand.

The phone rang. Three times. Then she picked up.

"Hello?" at the sound of her voice, my heart leapt and everything shifted to be right in the world.

"Hi, Abby. It's Hannah."

CHAPTER FIFTEEN

"YOU'RE making dinner?" Wayne asked, coming into the kitchen the next day.

"Yes, I thought I'd try one of your recipes, though I don't know why I bother. You're the gourmet chef. Things are not going well."

"That's probably because you followed the recipe. I never do."

"You could have told me that! I've been trying to get this thing to work all day while you've been at work! I wanted to do something special for you!"

"Here, let me take a look." Wayne lifted the lid on the steaming raviolis. After adding a little salt to the pot, he then tasted my sauce. Without a word, he started stirring in an assortment of spices.

I felt like crying yet again. In frustration, I took off the apron I was wearing, tossed in on the table and walked out of the room. I knew I must look exactly like the crazy person I felt I was. I'd tried so hard to make that recipe work. Handmade raviolis are not easy. I rubbed at the flour and sauce splattered across my sweat pants. Wayne and I hadn't bothered investing in new clothes for me since every day for the past month we'd been expecting me to be gone. Besides, I don't know that I could have drummed up the energy to dress in anything better than the supply of Wayne's sweatpants and T-shirts.

I went to the restroom to wash my hands and stare at my reflection in the mirror. My wavy auburn hair was sticking out at about a million different angles from the sloppy pony tail I'd tied with one of Wayne's shoelaces I'd found lying around. I was pale with dark circles under my blue eyes. Whenever I did manage to get back to my own time, my husband probably wouldn't recognize the person I'd become, let alone still want me!

I was so angry with myself! Angry that I couldn't pull myself together enough to get back to the right time. Angry that I was letting myself become so depressed it affected my appearance and everything else. Angry that I'd lost control and time traveled in the first place. And, finally, angry that I'd messed up the stupid ravioli!

I left the bathroom and the angry woman in the mirror behind, intent on flopping down on my perpetually-made bed on the couch and burying my face in my pillow.

Wayne met me as he was coming out of the kitchen. "The ravioli is going to be fine, Hannah. You didn't ruin it. Thank you for trying to do something special for me."

I nodded, but my eyes started burning anyway, and I turned away.

"Hannah, please," Wayne moaned. "Don't cry. I don't think I can take it if you cry."

"I'm sorry," I gulped. "I just can't seem to do anything

right. I'm stuck here getting on your nerves, and I can't even manage to make dinner right. And now I'm crying yet again. All I ever seem to do is cry. I'm sorry."

"Hannah, no. That's not what I was talking about." Wayne closed his eyes, took a deep breath, and then opened them to look directly at me, his eyes intense and seeming to sear right through me. "If you start crying, I won't be able to stop myself. I'll forget everything, take you in my arms, and kiss you until all the pain goes away."

I stared at him, completely shocked. "But I'm married!" I choked out.

"But you aren't married right now! The Hannah that I know, the Hannah of this time, is not married. Don't you think I've stared at your wedding ring every night for the past month? I vowed a long time ago that I wouldn't do anything to come in between you and my best friend, no matter how I felt, but I don't know how much more I can take. Hannah, I love you. I always have. And every day you're here cooking my dinner, wearing my clothes, being *you*... It just makes me fall deeper in love with you."

"I love Seth," I said. "I may not be married in this time, but I am a year from now. And right now, I miss him so much it hurts."

"I know you don't love me, Hannah. But I also know that it's taking me every ounce of strength I have to not at least try to make the Hannah of this time love me. I mean, you are the same person, and it's almost impossible for me to differentiate you into two distinct people. I know you're engaged, but you aren't married yet. If I told you how I felt, if I told you that I was madly, deeply, hopelessly in love with you, maybe it would make a difference. Maybe you would give me a chance and love me instead. I know it would ruin my friendship with Seth and completely mess up the timeline as you know it. I'm not the type of guy to steal his best friend's girl. But each day that passes, I fall deeper in love with you and get that much closer to saying 'screw it all' and at least trying to win your love."

I sank down on the couch, my legs suddenly too weak to support me. "Natalie mentioned once that she thought you were in love with me, but I didn't take her seriously. Have you always felt this way?"

"Yes. I mean, how could I not be attracted to you? You were the beautiful, mysterious woman who showed up to rescue me from making the most terrible mistake of my life. And then, when I compared you to Katherine, there was no competition. I've been able to keep things under control for years. I knew from the beginning that you were in love with Seth. I couldn't take my best friend's girl, even though I secretly hoped you two would break up. But now, I can't imagine the thought of actually watching the woman I love marry someone else."

"Does Seth have any idea how you feel?"

"We've never discussed it, but I think he suspects. I'm sure he sees the way I look at you. I know I can't completely hide how I feel, no matter how hard I try. There's a tension between us sometimes that I'm sure he feels. I mean, we did get in a fist fight over you once. But he also knows that I'm very loyal to him and wouldn't go behind his back. And I still wouldn't. If I were to make a try for you, I'd tell him. I'd tell him how I feel and hope that he would forgive me even though I had every intention of making his fiancé fall in love with me instead of him."

This was something I'd never considered. I'd never thought staying with Wayne could cause such potentially disastrous consequences. I didn't think he'd have a chance with the Hannah of this time, but he was the second most handsome, most wonderful man I'd ever known. If he played his cards right, he probably still wouldn't win me, but he would for sure destroy his relationship with Seth, putting the Tomorrow Foundation and everything they'd worked for in jeopardy.

"Hannah, did you ever think that maybe you did time travel for a reason this time? Maybe you were supposed to come back here so we could spend time together and I could fall more in love with you. Maybe I'm supposed to fight for you. Maybe God wants us to be together."

I shook my head, standing up from the couch and looking at him with all the determination I could muster. "No, Wayne. You can't do this. I'm in love with Seth, and I always have been. Nothing you can do will change that. I won't love you in any timeline. It will just ruin your relationship with Seth and everything you've worked for. Please, Wayne, I'm not worth it. Don't love me." A sob caught in my throat, making my voice waver on the last line.

Wayne looked deep in my eyes, and I couldn't look away. I knew he saw exactly what I was trying to do and also saw what a fragile hold I had on my control. I was shaking and almost afraid to breathe for fear my brave, determined façade would crumble into a mass of tears.

Wayne moved forward, closing in on me as if a magnet was drawing him. He stopped mere inches from my face. His eyes scanned my disheveled hair, my wet eyes, and my trembling lips.

His eyes were compassionate and held so much love. I

wanted to look away, but I couldn't.

"I'm going to leave now," he whispered. "If I stay even one more minute, I won't be able to stop myself from kissing you and proving to you just how wrong you are."

I was awakened by the sound of Wayne rummaging around in the kitchen. I glanced at the glowing red numbers on the digital clock sitting on the end table beside the couch. It was 2:00 in the morning. Wayne had been gone a long time. I had eaten the ravioli by myself, though I'd been so preoccupied with my thoughts I had barely recognized that it was delicious.

I heard Wayne getting out what I imagined was the ravioli I'd put in a container in the fridge. Then I heard the microwave start. I remained perfectly still, not wanting to alert him to the fact that I was awake. I didn't know what to say to him. When I thought about it, there didn't seem to be anything much left to say. He was in love with me. The longer I stayed, the greater chance there was that he would do something to try to break up Seth and me. I felt so helpless! I needed to find a way to get back to my own time and my husband, but this latest development just increased my stress level.

If I could have left Wayne's house and stayed somewhere else, I would have, but I had no other place to go. So, feeling miserable, I'd just gotten ready for bed, figuring I'd at least be asleep before Wayne arrived home.

How had I missed that Wayne had loved me all these years? I thought back over our entire relationship, now viewing every interaction with new eyes. Had there been clues that I had just missed, or had I been in denial of the obvious?

I thought back to my wedding. Wayne had said he didn't think he could watch me marry someone else, but in the original timeline, he'd been Seth's best man! I closed my eyes against the soft glow from the kitchen and let my mind drift back to my wedding day.

We had wanted to have the wedding ceremony in a church, so we had found a beautiful little chapel near the ocean. Our family and friends had barely fit in. Abby had been my matron of honor, of course, and Natalie and Seth's sister, Debra, had also been bridesmaids. They had all looked beautiful dressed in their knee-length pale blue sundresses and carrying yellow flowers.

My wedding dress had fit my dream perfectly. It had small, slightly off the shoulder straps that extended to a slight v neckline. The bodice was fitted all the way down past my hips. Then it flared out gradually into a full chapel length train. It was classic and simple, and from the look on Seth's face when I appeared with my dad at the end of the aisle, I gathered that he very much approved.

The ceremony had passed quickly in the chapel. I know the little sanctuary had been decorated with white and pale blue chiffon interspersed between yellow daisies and blue forget-me-nots, but all I really remembered was the look on Seth's face as he'd said his vows. He'd looked at me with such unimaginable love and said the words with such deep conviction. He was marrying me with no reservations. He was marrying me for life. Fifty years from now, that look on his face is what I would remember from my wedding ceremony.

The reception had been at Seth's parent's house, just a

short drive away from the chapel. My mind once again entered that beautiful backyard overlooking the ocean. I walked between white-cloaked tables decorated with yellow and blue flowers. I smelled the aroma of the catered food as it intermingled with the fresh sea breeze. I felt Seth's warm hand in mine as he led me around, greeting guests. And then I saw Wayne, dressed in his tux and standing away from the other guests as he leaned against a tree.

He had joined the rest of the guests as we cut the cake, and he gave a beautiful speech for the traditional toast. But now, in my mind, I studied his face. As my memories drifted, I once again heard the words.

"I guess I should talk about how Seth McAllister has been my best friend since the first day of college. I guess I should mention that he is like a brother to me and has challenged me, encouraged me, and even tried to beat me up if he felt the need. I guess I should say that he is a man of integrity with an intelligence second only to my own, of course. I guess I should say that Hannah is a lucky woman to get my best friend as her husband. But I'm not going to say that. For as incredible as Seth is, he is nothing when compared to his beautiful new wife. I would like to raise a toast to Seth and Hannah. May your years together be filled with much happiness and sprinkled with many blessings. And Seth, may you forever know how very lucky you are to have won Hannah's love."

Wayne had said all the right words, in exactly the right tone, but his eyes held a pain I hadn't recognized before. And as he raised his glass to drink, I noticed he seemed to have a little difficulty swallowing. Amid the cheers, Wayne slipped away, returning once again to catch the garter. He joked and posed for pictures with a smile plastered on his face, but it never reached his dull eyes.

As we were finally getting ready to make our dash for the waiting Rolls Royce, I turned to Seth, "Where is Wayne? I wanted to thank him and tell him goodbye."

"I think he already left," Abby said from beside me. I saw him walking back around the house to his car.

"He left already?" I asked, incredulous. "Why?"

"He probably had an appointment at a well-stocked bar," Natalie muttered.

I shot her a confused look. What was she talking about? Although, I couldn't say it was unusual to be confused by one of Natalie's cryptic comments.

"Don't worry, Hannah, I already talked to him," Seth reassured. "He set everything up for our departure, but he had to leave early to take care of some business."

"Yeah, the business of getting smashing drunk," I heard Natalie say under her breath. What was she talking about? Wayne didn't even drink!

At Seth's irritated glance, Natalie clammed up.

"He's got a lot on his plate at the office since he's covering for me while we're on our honeymoon," Seth explained.

I nodded. "Natalie, if you see him at some point, would you tell him 'thank you' for me?"

"Sure," Natalie replied. "I was planning on checking in with him later tonight anyway."

After quick hugs all around, Seth and I had made our escape through the rose petals and birdseed. I hadn't really given Wayne another thought.

The sound of Wayne's plate in the sink startled me from my thoughts. Revisiting my wedding had almost been like a dream, except the events hadn't been a product of my imagination.

All of my memories suddenly had new meaning as I realized how difficult it must have been for Wayne to watch me marry his best friend. I had been so wrapped up in my own happiness; I had missed the subtle details of Wayne's true feelings. Now my heart broke a little for this man and the unrequited love I could never return.

The light in the kitchen flipped off, and I heard Wayne's footsteps as he came through the living room, headed for the stairs. He paused as he passed the couch, and I knew he was watching me. I remained perfectly still and focused on keeping my breathing slow and even, as if I was asleep.

After several long moments, Wayne continued on up to the stairs. I waited until I heard the click of his bedroom door shutting, then I turned over, buried my head in my pillow, and prayed until sleep overtook me.

CHAPTER SIXTEEN

I had an idea. It was awful. It broke every rule possible in the ethics of time travel. It had the potential to be extremely dangerous and thoroughly screw up the timeline beyond repair.

And I was going to do it.

As usual, Wayne was gone to work when I woke in the morning. At least he wouldn't be around to talk me out of it.

The way I saw it, I didn't really have a choice. Staying here with Wayne was not an option. It would just make things worse and increase the chance that he would follow through with his desire to win me. In my mind, the danger of staying outweighed the danger of breaking a few rules to get me back where I belonged.

I just hoped I wasn't too late. I prayed Wayne hadn't reached the point of no return where he was determined to reveal his feelings to both Seth and me. Hopefully, if I just disappeared and made it home today, Wayne would leave the timeline alone and the next year would play out as it should.

As I'd lain in bed last night, I'd suddenly realized that I'd been wrong about Wayne being the only person who could help me. There was another person, and this person, more than anyone else, would understand exactly what I was going through.

I picked up the phone and stared at it. "God, please help me to not be making a mistake with this!"

Then, before I could second-guess myself, I dialed my own number.

The line picked up on the second ring.

"Hello?'

"Hi, Hannah. This is… Hannah. I'm having some time issues right now, and I'm a bit stuck. I know it's dangerous for me to call you, but I'm desperate. I need your help, and I thought you… I… could handle the weirdness."

The other Hannah was silent for a full ten seconds. "Okay," she said hesitantly. "So I guess this means I time travel again."

"You know I can't give you any information. And you can't mention this conversation to anyone, including Seth. Altering your behavior in any way could seriously mess things up for me… you. You pretty much need to forget this ever happened."

"I understand."

It was more than a little strange to hear my own voice on the other end of the line and to realize that I was actually talking to another version of myself. And the good thing was, the universe hadn't collapsed yet.

"You said we're stuck?" the other Hannah asked.

"What can I do to help?"

"I have a plan. I just need you to bring me my… your… our art kit."

"Okay. Where do I take it?"

"Just take it to Wayne's townhouse and leave it on the front porch. Don't go inside or anything, and don't mention it to Wayne."

"I'll be there as soon as I can."

I gasped as an image suddenly entered my mind. It was a memory of me placing my art case to the left of Wayne's door, turning around and leaving. It was a new memory, one I'd just created, but that had happened, for me, in the past. I'd created new memories before, but never with something so immediate. I quickly searched my brain for any other new memories, trying to figure out if this act had caused any other diversions in the timeline. No. There was nothing. I never mentioned the phone call to Seth or Wayne, and I still went back in time on my honeymoon.

"Good girl, Hannah," I said, reassured that she would perform her tasks well. Then I hung up.

Fifteen minutes later, I heard a noise at the front door. Peeking out of a slit in the blinds, I saw the back of my own head as she / I walked back to my SUV parked on the street.

I waited a full minute after the other Hannah had driven away. Then I opened the door and retrieved the large briefcase that held my highest quality art supplies.

This was going to work. I knew it. But there was one other thing I needed to do before I left.

I walked back over to the phone and dialed.

"Hello?"

"Hi, Abby. It's Hannah."

I'd called Abby several times over the past month. The sound of her voice, alive and well never ceased to thrill me. I'd never called to do anything other than talk. And we'd never discussed anything other than the mundane. I was careful. Abby didn't have caller ID, so in her mind, I was just regular Hannah calling to chat, yet I didn't mention anything that she would ever need to continue discussing with the other Hannah. I never said anything or gave any information that might change the course of history, and Abby had never revealed any deeper secrets or anything that I didn't already know. I liked to call just to hear her voice.

But consequences or no consequences, I couldn't leave this time without at least trying to save my sister's life. I knew it was probably highly illegal in Wayne's mind and in the official time travel constitution, but I didn't care. I didn't pray about it, and I didn't ask God's permission, because honestly, I didn't want to know what He thought on the matter. I didn't want to risk Him disagreeing with me. I could not let her die when I could possibly prevent it with a few well-placed words.

"Hi, Hannah! What's up? Can I call you back? I'm right in the middle of trying to get lunch for the Silver Springs guests. We're having a busy week with the skiers."

"Oh, don't bother calling me back. I just have a quick, rather bizarre request."

"Okay. What is it?"

Could you come stay with me for a couple days next December 18th? Don't forget. Even if I don't mention it again, I want you to come surprise me on December 18th."

"I guess I could come. It's not as if I have anything scheduled on that day this far out. What is this about?"

"It's just a silly idea I have. But it would really mean a lot to me. Do you promise? Will you come visit me December 18th? Mark it on your calendar."

"Sure. I'll do that. Gotta run. I'll talk to you later."

Abby hung up.

I pushed the 'end' button, not completely satisfied with the phone call. Abby was too smart and too nosey to let me get away with a cryptic request like that. She had obviously been distracted. There was nothing I could do about it though. Hopefully, Abby would do like she said by marking it on the calendar and following through. She would die on December 19, but if she came and stayed with me on December 18, she would never fight with Tom and never drive down that road the next day. When I did manage to get back to my own today, I wanted to find my sister alive and waiting for me.

I had already changed my clothes back into the blouse, skirt, and pumps I'd arrived in. Now, I donned my coat, quickly scribbled a note to Wayne and grabbed the cash from the counter. When I had first arrived at his house, Wayne had given me some emergency cash in case I needed to run to the store for something. I hadn't ever needed it since I'd never stepped outside the house except when he was with me, but now I took both it and the house key lying on the breakfast bar.

I walked out the door, locked it behind me, and went to the corner to catch the bus. I'd already checked the schedule using Wayne's computer. A short time later, I was in Golden Gate Park looking out at the bridge spanning across Stowe Lake.

I set up the supplies and the small easel I carried in my art kit. As I moved to sit down, I suddenly realized that maybe it hadn't been such a good idea to wear my skirt. I positioned the art case to use as a sort of stool to perch on. Then I managed to move my legs comfortably to the side and began getting my paints ready. Sitting on the case was necessary anyway. If my plan worked as I hoped, I'd be time traveling. I had to maintain physical contact with anything I wanted to come with me. And there was no way I wanted to leave my art case behind.

I picked up my paintbrush, loving how it fit in my hand like a comfortable old shoe. There was a reason I'd needed this particular art kit. I couldn't go to the store and get just any art supplies. These were mine. They were old friends that I had gathered over the years. The other Hannah would have to do without our art kit for a year, but she wouldn't be needing it. She was going to be too busy with getting married and the Master's program. I didn't remember the last time I'd gotten to spend time with the friends in my art case.

I took a deep breath and looked at the beautiful scene in front of me. The light was diffused as it came through the trees, casting shadows and reflecting mirror images in the still water. The stone bridge almost looked like something out of colonial America as it arched gracefully across the serene water. The park was in the middle of the city, and yet it was so quiet. The only sound was the gentle splashing of some ducks at the water's edge.

As my paintbrush made the first stroke across the canvas, I felt like I could suddenly breathe. I'd forgotten how therapeutic art was for me. With the simple feel of the brush in my hand, I felt right. I felt whole. Art had always been my happy place. No matter what was going on in my life, I could start drawing or painting and all the tension I carried in my muscles would suddenly dissipate. As I focused on matching the color of the leaves in the water's reflection, the rest of the world faded away. I took my time, painting the bridge, the trees, and the sliver of blue sky overhead. In the foreground, I painted the delicate, lacy branches of a tree draping itself into the scene from the left. Then, finally, I painted a woman down by the water's edge. She was blond and wearing a long, flowing white dress. As I added the highlights to her hair where the sun caught the golden locks, I paused, looking at the small figure I had painted. I realized it was Abby.

I added the finishing touches to Abby's picture, making sure the shadows had enough depth and the sun was casting its soft glow at the right angle.

I don't know how long I had sat there painting. I usually didn't complete a painting all in one setting. Normally I would do a rough outline at the actual setting and then take it home to slave over for days or maybe even weeks. But for this one, I lost track of time, and finishing it was almost a compulsion. My back had grown stiff, and I'd had to shift my position several times since my legs kept falling asleep. But still I'd painted.

My paintbrush finally stopped. I looked at Abby standing by the peaceful lake, and I felt blessedly empty—like I'd poured every ounce of grief and love onto that canvas and there was nothing left. It was the same wonderful emptiness, the same release that comes after a good, long cry. Every tear had been shed, every pent-up emotion had now been exhausted.

I felt a presence behind me a split second before he spoke.

"Hannah."

I turned to find Seth.

Before I could say a word, he scooped me up in his arms and crushed me to him. He showered gentle kisses all over my face, and then he claimed my lips with both a desperation and a joy that was breathtaking.

Suddenly he stopped, released me and handed me a small white pill.

"Quick, stick this under your tongue and let it dissolve."

I did as he instructed. But the dizziness I'd attributed to his kisses remained.

"I think I need to sit down," I said, sinking back down to the grass. "Don't you have a shot for me?"

"That was Karisenol I just gave you. It'll work quickly since it dissolves under the tongue. If you don't feel better in the next minute, I'll give you an injection."

"You created an oral version of the Karisenol?"

Seth shrugged, "Yeah, I've had a bit of time on my hands lately, and a lot of excess worry." He bent down beside me and scanned my face. "Are you okay?"

I knew he was referring to more than just the dizziness. I nodded. "I think the Karisenol is working." I rather pointedly didn't answer the broader question. I didn't know. I'd been doing awful for a month, and now? I was back in my own time, but I still couldn't seem to assess exactly how I was doing.

"I'm sorry, Seth," I said quietly. "I was stuck and couldn't get back. I can only imagine what you've been through the past month, not knowing where I'd gone and if I'd return."

"It's okay, Hannah, there's nothing you could have done. Thankfully, after you'd been gone about three days, Wayne told me that you'd traveled back a year and you'd been with him. So at least I knew that you were safe, and I also knew when you'd return."

"I'm so glad he told you. I was afraid he would wait until it was time for me to return."

"I think that was his original plan. He was worried about messing up the timeline or something. But then he quickly realized he couldn't wait. I wasn't handling your disappearance well, and your mom was inconsolable. I don't think I was able to eat or sleep for those first few days. Wayne was afraid I wouldn't make it a week, let alone over a month, if he didn't tell me. He also told me exactly when and where you'd be back, saying that when you finally did make it, you'd left him a note telling him to have me meet you here."

I was quiet, staring back over the lake and my painting. "I don't seem to have any new memories, so I already know the answer. Abby is still dead, isn't she?"

"Yes, Hannah," Seth said gently, fear evident in his eyes. The poor man was probably living in fear that I would get upset and travel once again. "She died December 19th."

I nodded. "Then nothing has changed. I'd asked her to come visit me on the 18th, but I guess that didn't happen."

"No, she didn't come."

"Is my mom okay?" I asked, needing to change the subject. I didn't want to keep thinking about Abby and clutter up my mind with grief again after I'd just emptied it.

"She was able to pull things together once we told her where and when you were and when you'd be back. She and your dad are waiting for you back at the apartment. She wanted to come, but we didn't want to overwhelm you right away with a welcoming party."

Seth reached out and gently caressed my face. I closed my eyes, just enjoying his touch. When I finally opened them, I found him staring at me with indescribable love and sorrow.

"Hannah, I don't know that I can take it if you do this to me again," he whispered brokenly. "Even though Wayne told me you were fine and said you'd pretty much just sat around his house for a month waiting to be beamed out of there, I was still completely lost without you. If you hadn't been able to get to Wayne, if you hadn't figured out how to get yourself back here… there's so much that could've gone wrong. I don't know how I'm going to live knowing you could be ripped away from me at any time."

I was touched by his honesty. Seth was always the strong one, but the past month must have broken something in him. He was now revealing a vulnerability he tended to keep hidden.

I scooted over and sat in his lap with my arms around his neck and my head on his shoulder. Oh, he felt good! I had missed him so much. It was almost as if I was being reunited with a limb of my body. I had felt incomplete without him.

"I know it isn't going to be easy, Seth, but if you think about it, we're not really different than any other couple. There are no guarantees in life. At any time, one of us could die. Look at Abby. When she woke up on December 19th, she had no idea she would die that day. I'm sure Tom felt like she'd been ripped away from him."

"I guess you're right," Seth said, cradling me close. "That still doesn't make it any easier though. It's going to take me a while to get over the trauma from this past month."

"It's going to take me some time to recover too. Right now, the thought of time traveling again is enough to give me a panic attack." A shudder went through me from head to toe. "I'll try to do better. I should have kept better control at the funeral. If I had, none of this would have happened."

"It's not your fault, Hannah. Your sister had died. We knew it would be a miracle for you to make it through the grief without time traveling."

I thought back to the funeral, remembering the hopelessness and desperation that had gripped me as I'd tried to say goodbye.

"It is my fault. I had other people there with me. I could have accepted all of your help and comfort, but I pushed everyone away, trying to deal with it on my own. Grandma was right there with me. I could have turned to her. Oh my goodness, how is Grandma? Did you have to tell her about my time travel? She probably saw me disappear!"

"She didn't see it," Seth assured. "She'd turned away

to give you a moment of privacy. When she turned back around, you were gone. She was very upset. Of course, your parents and I knew you had time traveled. We tried to invent some excuses, saying you'd probably gone with a friend, but your grandma is too smart. We tried outright lying to her and pretended that you'd called me on the phone and said you were visiting a friend for a few days. I don't think she bought that either. After a few days, though, she seemed to let it go and be okay with the idea that you were visiting a friend and would be back in about a month. Your mom must have added some other details to convince her."

"That's a relief. I've been worried that Grandma would be torturing herself over 'losing' me."

"Oh, she did the first day. But no more so than the rest of us. Thankfully, though, she seemed to recover. I think Natalie might have helped with that. Your mom hatched some sort of elaborate plan to make it appear that you were with Natalie in some exotic, healing location. Natalie was only too willing to use her acting skills, even though she didn't know and didn't want to know the reasons why her services were needed."

"That sounds like Natalie," I said with a smile. Natalie may lack information about a project, but she was never lacking enthusiasm. Hopefully one day I'd be able to explain everything to her, though I would be very happy if I didn't need to add any more installments in my saga after this one. Before, I had feared time traveling because of the potentially deadly repercussions on my body. Although the physical effects of time traveling were still a very real fear, even with the Karisenol, I now also feared getting stuck again in the wrong time. What if I wasn't able to get back home the next time?

My gaze wandered back to my painting. I was so glad it had come with me. I'm not sure I could have coped had it been left on the other side of my time travel.

Seth's gaze followed mine, and he spoke softly, "It's a beautiful painting, Hannah. Maybe your best."

I remained silent. I'd succeeded in returning to my today, but it still wasn't the today I wanted.

"Come on, Hannah. Let's get you home." Seth stood, seemingly eager to get me away from the sudden shift of my mood to melancholy. I could tell we were going to have a long road ahead of us. I would still need to work through my grief, and yet Seth was going to be fearful every time I shed a tear.

I gathered up my paint brushes and put them away while Seth chattered on, trying his best to lift my attitude. "I'm sure your mom has already made dinner for us and is probably pacing the floor waiting for you."

Seth carried the case and I carried the painting. As Seth's silver BMW came into view, I saw a tall figure leaning against it. Even from a distance, I recognized Wayne.

His car was parked next to Seth's, though it was Seth's luxury car he was lounging on. He straightened as we approached.

"Hey, McAllister," he greeted. "I was just checking to make sure Hannah made it back okay and you didn't manage to lose her again or anything."

"No chance of that," Seth replied with a smile. Wayne and Seth were constantly giving each other a hard time over anything and everything. "From now on, I'm going to be watching her so closely, she's going to be lucky if I let her use the bathroom by herself."

"Yes, because using the bathroom is a highly emotional experience," I said dryly.

"It's good to see you, Hannah," Wayne said seriously, meeting my eyes with his sober ones.

I searched his face. In the last conversation I'd had with him, he'd confessed his love for me and threatened to attempt to break my engagement with Seth. But for him, that same conversation had been a year ago. While studying his face, I also searched my memory for anything different. Had he followed through or had he kept his silence? Did he do anything to change the original timeline as I remembered it?

There was pain behind his eyes, but it was the lonely kind of pain one kept hidden. Wayne's mouth parted in a sad smile. He knew exactly what I was doing.

I sighed in relief, and yet I was still bothered. Wayne had kept his silence. It had obviously been at great personal cost to himself, but he had done nothing. And I knew he'd done it out of love for me. I had asked him not to, so he had stood silently by and watched me marry his best friend.

"Thank you, Wayne," I breathed quietly. "For everything."

Wayne shrugged, his brown eyes glinting in a sudden mischievous twinkle. "Maybe in another place or time, Hannah."

I laughed. "Ugh. Sorry, Wayne, but I certainly hope

not."

Seth was looking at us curiously, but he didn't bother to ask for clarification.

"Come on, Wayne. You can talk Hannah's ear off tomorrow at work. If I don't get her back to our apartment soon, my mother-in-love is going to have my head."

Wayne walked with me around to the other side of the car and held the passenger's side door open while Seth climbed into the driver's side.

As I moved past him to get in, Wayne sighed dramatically and said, "Well, Hannah, no matter what happens, I guess we can say we'll always have ravioli."

I laughed, delighted that, despite everything, Wayne was still Wayne. I couldn't imagine anyone else I'd rather share ravioli with.

CHAPTER SEVENTEEN

I adjusted the graduation cap atop my head and turned to look at my mom.

"What do you think?" I asked self-consciously. Mom was helping me get ready for my graduation ceremony. With my gown over my dress and my flat hat in position, I was as ready as I was going to be, though I was a bit nervous about the hat's precarious perch.

"I'm so proud of you, Hannah," Mom said, forgetting her job as my fashion consultant as she tried to hold back her tears. "I know these last five months have been awful. But look at you! You still managed to finish your Master's program, and now you're graduating!"

"You make it sound like more of an accomplishment than it is, Mom," I said. "When I got back in January, I'd only missed a week of the session. Honestly, having this program to finish is probably the only thing that has kept me sane. Otherwise, I wouldn't have had anything to take my mind off Abby. Now that I'm actually done, I'm not sure what I'll do."

"Don't worry, Seth and Wayne will keep you plenty

busy at the Foundation. Besides, the grief is probably a bit more manageable now as opposed to five months ago. At least, it is for me. I'm not on the bed writhing in pain anymore. I still have my moments, but as a whole, I can function now. I'm not sure if time heals all wounds, but it at least makes them more bearable."

I was glad to see that my mom was beginning to heal. But the truth was, I wasn't. I still felt that agony every time I thought of Abby. I hadn't been dealing with her death. I had pretty much stalled in the grief process and had been very effectively distracting myself from thinking about it. Seth, probably terrified of me becoming emotional, hadn't pushed me to deal with the grief, but had even seemed to encourage my state of denial.

Overall, he had managed to keep things remarkably uneventful since January. He'd found a good balance of being completely honest with me but also being cautious about upsetting me. While I didn't really like the cautious part, I knew it couldn't really be avoided. He loved me and didn't want to lose me again. I just appreciated that he was still making a concerted effort at honesty. He'd kept me informed on all his projects at work, including the project with the anti-depressants. There really hadn't been much to report, though. Seth had made a few contacts who were gathering information and making preparations while he quietly continued research.

I also appreciated that he hadn't tried to shield me from his real emotions. Though I often felt like he held back a bit, he still loved me with passion, teased me with great delight, and got upset with me fairly often. The only subject he consistently steered clear of was Abby. I had never asked for his help in dealing with it or talking it out, and I think he'd been too afraid to confront me about my grief.

So now we were leaving for my graduation ceremony in just a few moments, and although I was happy to be walking in the ceremony, I was also terrified of what would happen afterward. With no Master's degree goal to occupy me, would I actually have to deal with the fact that my sister was dead?

"I don't know, Mom," I said thoughtfully. I really wanted to confide in her, but did I dare let her know how much I was still struggling? "I know it's been five months, but sometimes I still feel angry with God that He let her die," I admitted softly. "At other times, I blame myself."

"Hannah, why in the world would you blame yourself? You had nothing to do with Abby's accident."

"Maybe if I had answered her call that morning…"

"Hannah, it is not your fault," Mom said firmly. "I can understand being angry with God. That's completely normal. I certainly don't understand why He let my baby die. I don't know that I ever will. But that's not the point. Even though I don't understand, even though I still feel angry sometimes, even though I will never get over losing her, even though… I will still trust Him. Look at your own life, Hannah. The God who so meticulously arranged your life, knows what He's doing, even in this. I don't have to understand or like it, but I do have to let God carry me through it and use it to bring Him whatever glory He intends. I'm not willing for Abby's death to be wasted. I want to be in on God's plan."

"I know in my head that what you're saying is true, Mom, but in my heart, Abby's death still feels so wrong. If I accept it, if I let her go and let God have His way, it would be like saying that it was right. I should have been there for her when she'd called. I feel like I let her down, and if I accept her death, I feel like I'd be letting her down again. I mean, I can time travel! God used me to save an entire family single-handedly! And yet I couldn't manage to save my sister."

"I picked up the phone when she called, Mom," I admitted softly. "But I was busy. I saw it was Abby, and I chose not to answer it. I thought I could call her later."

"Hannah, this is not your fault and it is not your responsibility. You didn't know Abby was going to die. Chances are, answering that phone call wouldn't have changed a thing. Abby is gone, and she is in a much better place. You are not doing Abby any favors with your guilt. It's God's responsibility to make sense out of this, not yours. You can't change it. You couldn't save Abby five months ago, and you certainly can't go back and save her now. It's not as if you can control when and where you time travel. God's the one who controls it and ordains when you go and what you do. He is in control of this too."

At my mother's words, it was as if I'd just witnessed the birth of a star in the night sky. Where there once was nothing, a pinprick of light had suddenly appeared, growing stronger and illuminating shadowy areas I'd never known existed.

Something of my epiphany must have shown on my face.

"Hannah, what did I say?" Mom asked cautiously.

"You're right, Mom," I said quickly, trying to cover my reaction. "I'm not doing any favors for Abby or her memory. The way I've been feeling has been almost paralyzing to me. I guess I need to let go of some things and focus on getting on with my life and being more proactive."

Mom still seemed skeptical. Even though I tried to smile in reassurance, I still recognized uncertainty and a glint of fear in her eyes.

"Okay, ladies, are we ready to get Hannah graduated?" Seth asked, entering the room. He had apparently tired of waiting for us to emerge. With the clock warning that it was time to leave, he'd come to find us himself.

Shooting a nervous look my direction, Mom followed Seth out to head for the car.

I followed them as well, but as I passed my calendar on the wall, I paused, looking at it.

It was May. Abby had died on December 19th.

"It's not as if you can control when and where you time travel."

I always traveled back to the same day, just a different year. I always traveled to the same place I'd left from. Extreme emotion is what triggered me to leap through time. I had never been able to control it, but I'd never tried. What if, for just once, I didn't want to prevent it? What if I actually *wanted* to time travel?

If I could send myself back in time…

I could change December 19th.

As my thoughts whirled with ideas and plans, I couldn't stop the slow smile.

And for the first time in five months, I felt peace.

TRANSLATION KEY

HANNAH'S friend, Natalie, is British and tends to use British slang when nervous or upset. So if you feel like you might be 'having kittens' one day, and would like to try Natalie's method of managing stress, here are a few phrases you will recognize from the book!

Bolt hole - a place where you can hide, especially to escape.

Chocks away - here we go!

Having kittens - to become extremely upset, nervous, or anxious. Freaking out, or losing it. Similar to the US phrase 'having a cow.'

Mums - moms.

Smashing - terrific.

Today Timeline

G

F

2. Abby dies. Hannah travels back 1 year.
1. While on her honeymoon, Hannah travels back 1 year.

I

E

C

B

A

Note:
Every time Hannah
changes something in
the past, the timeline is
skewed and a new,
altered future is created.
The previous timeline
ceases to exist.

'Yesterday' begins here.

Previous Events in the Yesterday series:

A - After traveling back 5 years, Hannah saves the Lawsons.
B - Hannah saves Wayne. Seth waits for her.
C - Hannah time travels with Seth into the past.
D - Hannah and Seth save Nicole Kraeger.
E - Hannah travels 35 years into the future.
F - Hannah meets Karis and tells her to send baby Hannah
    back in the time machine 59 years.
G - Karis and Jason send baby Hannah back in the time machine.
H - Baby Hannah arrives in the past and is adopted by the Kraegers.
I - Hannah saves Seth based on info from Karis's letter.

H

D

Original Timeline

READER'S GUIDE

WHILE the *Yesterday* series is a fantastic story filled with twists and excitement, it is also intended as an extra-ordinary example of the way God works in our lives to accomplish His purpose and mold us into who He wants us to be.

In *Today* I really wanted to play with the idea of what would happen to Hannah if she was a real person. Life usually isn't fair, and many times bad things happen. Hannah has the fantastic ability to time travel, but how would she react when faced with real-life scenarios of danger and loss?

Like in the other two books, *Today* is a continued illustration of Psalm 139, yet it takes the characters to a new depth where hopefully all readers can relate.

As you read this book, did you think about the way God works in your own life? Could you relate to Hannah's grief and anger? What about now? Can you look at the trials in your life and see God's hand molding you into the person He has called you to be? Can you identify your own mistakes and see their effect on your walk with God?

As you answer these questions and reflect on the book, may you see some of the beauty of God's work in your own life. I pray your fellowship and discussion blesses you in your relationship with God as you search the scripture, reflect, share, and pray. May the Lord draw you close to Him and give you comfort through all of your own trials and heartache. And may he also grant you hope for the future where His purpose is fulfilled. "For weeping may endure for the night, but joy comes in the morning." Psalm 30:5b

> *Your eyes saw my substance, being yet unformed. And in Your book they all were written, the days fashioned for me, when as yet there were none of them.*
>
> Psalm 139:16

While on her honeymoon, Hannah's sheer happiness causes her to time travel one year in the past, where she learns some important information but also has a series of embarrassing encounters.

1. Just for fun, think about some of your embarrassing moments from the past. Can you laugh about them yet?

2. Part of the reason I wanted to write this part about Hannah time traveling on her honeymoon was for the humor aspect. Much of the rest of the book is quite serious, so I wanted some comic relief at the beginning. What part of Hannah's awkward adventures in Hawaii did you find the most humorous?

When Hannah returns to her own time, she decides not to tell Seth about what she learned in the past regarding Katherine, Jones-Stanton Pharmaceudicals, and the attempt on his life. Hannah keeps it secret in an effort to protect her husband, but it results in damaging their relationship.

3. Have you ever tried to keep a secret from someone you loved? Can you relate to Hannah's reasons for doing so? Did your secret have a similar ending to Hannah's?

4. Have you ever had a secret kept from you? Can you relate to Seth's emotion when Hannah's secret was finally revealed? Did the secret have consequences to your relationships?

5. Maybe you don't have personal experience with keeping a secret or having one kept from you, but maybe you've witnessed the effects of secrets in the lives of others. What consequences have you seen? Have you ever witnessed something good resulting from a secret?

6. Discussion Question: If and when is it ever okay to keep a secret from someone?
Proverbs 11:3, Luke 6:31, Acts 24:16

Life is good at bringing the unexpected. I wanted the reader to feel the complete shock, raw emotion, and grief that Hannah felt when Abby died. One day, she is graduating, and she thought she knew what tomorrow held. Then, suddenly, life is never the same.

7. No one makes it through life unscathed. Everyone has felt the shock of an unexpected twist of life—a death, loss of a job, an accident, etc. In that moment, did you feel as Hannah does? How did you react?

8. Obviously, Hannah did not deal well with her grief, even through the end of the book. What helped you through your own tunnel of grief?

9. Looking at everything Hannah went through, what advice would you have given her? What do you think she should have done differently?

10. At the end of the book, do you think Hannah has finally come to terms with her grief of losing her sister? What, if any, problem areas do you think still exist in her attitude? What do you think the future holds for Hannah?

Job 1: 20-23, Job 42:2-3, Ecclesiastes 3:1-11

Hannah's reaction is a common one for someone experiencing intense grief. She is angry with God. After losing her sister, Hannah says:

I didn't say anything to Seth. What would he think if he knew I was developing an anger toward God? Seth was so strong and sure in his faith. Would he be shocked, maybe even repulsed, that I was blaming God? I felt almost ashamed but powerless to stop it. I knew God was real. I knew He was in control of absolutely everything. He was infinite, powerful, all-knowing. He supposedly loved me. I knew he could have easily protected my sister. He could have saved her. So how could I not be angry? He let her die.

11. Can you relate to what Hannah is feeling in this excerpt? Has there ever been a time when you felt angry at God? Maybe you've witnessed someone else's anger toward Him.

12. Was there anything that helped you get beyond the anger? Or maybe you are going through the gauntlet and struggling like Hannah.

Psalm 13:1-6, Psalm 42:9-11, Matthew 5:4

Hannah's faith undergoes a drastic change in this book. In the beginning, she is trusting God, praying for peace and protection, yet in the end, her relationship with Him has a new level of complexity.

I didn't pray about it, and I didn't ask God's permission, because honestly, I didn't want to know what He thought on the matter. I didn't want to risk Him disagreeing with me.

13. How would you describe the change in Hannah's faith? What is your experience with either yourself or others in a similar faith crisis?

14. Hannah still has a long journey ahead of her in terms of her faith. What do you think needs to happen in order for her to get back in right relationship with God?

Jeremiah 29:11, Isaiah 1:18, Isaiah 43:2

15. What about you? Are you or someone you know struggling with grief, anger, or faith issues? Please share so others can join in prayer.

Psalm 34:18

16. For those of you who have made it through grief, anger at God, or a testing of faith, let your testimony be an encouragement and share how God carried you through.

1 Corinthians 1:3-4

NOTES:

YESTERDAY SERIES

The Yesterday Series:

Book 1: Yesterday

Book 2: The Locket

Book 3: Today

Book 4: The Choice

Book 5: Tomorrow

Book 6: The Promise

FIND all the stories in the *Yesterday* series wherever fine books are sold.

MORE GREAT BOOKS

The Tru Exceptions Series:

Book 1: Baggage Claim

Book 2: Point of Origin

Book 3: Mirage

Stand-Alone Novels:

Secret Santa

The Romance of the Sugar Plum Fairy

Random Acts of Cupid

The Assumption of Guilt

SNEAK PEEK

ENJOY this special excerpt from *The Choice*, book 4 in the *Yesterday* series, available now wherever fine books are sold.

"SETH, could you please slow down?" I asked, trying to extract my fingernails from the dashboard of my SUV.

"Oh, I'm sorry. I didn't think you'd mind."

I looked at my husband like he was crazy. Mind? Why would I not mind? He was well-aware of my phobia of letting other people drive. But more than that, my sister had died on this same road almost a year ago to the day!

It was December 18th. Seth and I were going to Silver Springs to spend the holidays with my parents. We had also wanted to be together for the anniversary of Abby's death. Tomorrow would likely be a difficult day for the whole family, except for me. I wasn't planning on doing any more mourning. In fact, if everything went according to my plan, there would be no reason to mourn.

I was going to change December 19th.

I had spent the last seven months planning this, and yet I was still remarkably ill-prepared. I knew I wanted to time travel. I was going to purposely send myself back in time to save my sister. But I still hadn't quite decided on how.

My current plan was to get up early tomorrow morning and sneak out of the lodge to go skiing. I hate skiing. Mostly because I'm terrible at it. Just the thought of trying to go down one of the runs around Silver Springs was enough to send my heart into palpitations of fear—which is exactly what I needed to induce time travel.

Of course, nobody knew about my plan. And I wasn't going to tell Seth or anyone else. This was something I needed to do. If I told them, they would try to talk me out of it. I, more than anyone else, was fully aware of the risks. There was no guarantee that I would travel to a year ago. I might miss my target and go back further or even forward to a different December 19th. If I did manage to time travel, I might get stuck and not be able to return. Having already experienced that once, it was not something I'd want to repeat. And, finally, if I did travel to the right time, save Abby, and manage to return, I would face life-threatening side effects from the time travel.

And all that is not even taking into consideration the fact that I'd be messing around with time. I might really screw up history for myself, my family, or for the entire human race!

I knew that I might never see my husband again. I

knew that I might die. But those were 'mights,' and they paled in comparison to the alternative. If I didn't time travel, my sister would stay dead.

I watched out the window as the trees blurred past.

"Seth, you're going too fast again!" I said, darting a glance at the speedometer. When I had initially objected, Seth had obediently slowed. Now, however, his speed had gradually increased. But it was even more terrifying now that we were beginning to move through the curves as the road wound up to the resort my parents owned.

"I'm sorry, Hannah. I really didn't think you'd mind."

"What in the world are you talking about?" I fumed, aggravated that he'd used the same nonsensical explanation as before. "Of course I mind! You know the dangers of this road and how many people have been killed here!"

To Seth's credit, the roads were perfectly clear. My parents had done a great job of making sure the roads were safe for those traveling up to the resort. New guardrails had been put in place, and the roads were regularly plowed and sanded. Even though the snow lay in neat walls at the side of the road and there wasn't any ice even on the corners, I still didn't like the speed with which he was taking the curves. If I hadn't already been so paranoid, I would have insisted on being the driver.

Seth responded, "Fear, grief, anxiety, anger, happiness. I figured we might as well start with fear."

"What in the world are you talking about, Seth McAllister?"

"If you're intending to go back in time, you're going to need a way to get there. I figured if we scared you enough…"

I looked at Seth with my mouth open in shock. "I… how…" I stammered, both denial and questions on my lips.

"Come on, Hannah. I've known for months. Your mom told me about her conversation with you and how you reacted when she mentioned that you have no control over your time traveling. After that, your entire demeanor toward life changed. It didn't take much imagination to figure out what you'd decided to do."

I swallowed. There was no use denying it. "I have to do this, Seth. If there's even the smallest possibility that I could save her, I have to try."

"I'm not going to try to talk you out of it, Hannah," Seth said gently. "I'm sure you've already considered the risks and the sheer magnitude of what you're intending. But there is one other thing you need to consider. You know that the Hannahpren loses its effectiveness over time, which is why you still face the risk of time travel even though you take the daily medication. What Wayne and I haven't mentioned to you before is that Karisenol could have the same tendency. Over time, your body might not respond to it as well. Wayne and I are still trying to figure out how to adapt the medications, but right now, there's no guarantee that the Karisenol will save your life if you time travel. When you return, it might not be enough. You might die."

"Thank you for telling me, Seth, but that doesn't really change my mind. You're right in that I've already considered the risks. Dying is one that I've already come to terms with."

I saw pain flash through Seth's face. I knew that, in

many ways, I was actually being very selfish. I wanted to change history for my sake. I couldn't stand the idea of my sister being gone from my life forever. Because of that, I was willing to put Seth and my parents through the pain of having me disappear and possibly die.

Despite his obvious concern, Seth still spoke quietly. "You have a miraculous ability. It's only natural that you would want to use it to save someone you love. I just have one question for you, and then I'll leave you alone. Have you prayed about this? Do you really feel it is something God would have you do? You used to be so concerned about messing up what is supposed to be. Maybe God intends to use Abby's death in some other way to bring out good in your life."

I was silent. I had, very specifically, not prayed about this. And I had no intention of doing so. As bad as it sounded, I didn't want God's opinion. I didn't want to consider the possibility that He might not want me to do it.

While not directly answering the question, I still managed to reply. "Abby's death is not God's will. It can't be. Why would He give me this ability if he didn't want me to use it? I can't be at peace knowing that I could have the chance to save her."

"But what if you can't? What if you go back and make things worse? What if this isn't God's will? What if you're wrong? Are you really ready to take that responsibility if you're wrong?"

"I'm not wrong."

"Hannah, you've never tried to time travel before. It's always just happened. What you're doing is to purposely go back. It seems like you're trying to take the control out of God's hands. Are you sure this is a line you want to cross?"

"Seth, this is my choice. I'm going to go back and save her. I have to."

"Okay, then," Seth said simply.

The SUV suddenly accelerated. The curves in the road were coming fast, and I was being thrown first one way and then the other as Seth careened through the corners.

"Seth, what are you doing!" I shrieked.

"If you're determined to screw things up, I'm going to screw them up with you!"

"Seth, slow down! You're going to get us killed!"

"I will not slow! Either we die together or we time travel together, but you are not going to leave me again!"

ABOUT THE AUTHOR

AMANDA TRU loves to write exciting books with plenty of unexpected twists. She figures she loses so much sleep writing the things, it's only fair she makes readers lose sleep with books they can't put down!

Amanda has always loved reading, and writing books has been a lifelong dream. A vivid imagination helps her write captivating stories in a wide variety of genres. Her current book list includes everything from holiday romances, to action-packed suspense, to a Christian time travel / romance series.

Amanda is a former elementary school teacher who now spends her days being mommy to three little boys and her nights furiously writing. Amanda and her family live in a small Idaho town where the number of cows outnumber the number of people.

Connect with Amanda Tru online:
http://amandatru.blogspot.com/

CONNECT ONLINE

Author site:
http://amandatru.blogspot.com/

Newsletter email sign up:
http://eepurl.com/ZQdw9

Facebook:
https://www.facebook.com/amandatru.author

Twitter:
https://twitter.com/TruAmanda

GooglePlus+:
https://plus.google.com/+AmandaTru

Pinterest:
http://www.pinterest.com/truamanda/

Goodreads:
https://www.goodreads.com/author/show/5374686.Amanda_Tru